PRAISE FOR C

Conor Montague is a fearless writer with an uncanny ability to take the reader further, faster. Fierce, poetic, innovative and often very funny. This collection has it all; the depths and the darkness, as well as images that ring clear as a bell and linger. A brilliant body of work.
—Jess Kidd, author of *The Night Ship*

Flan O'Brien meets Hunter S – Fear and Loathing in Ballinasloe and beyond. Montague's wild book is akin to strapping yourself onto a rollercoaster that snakes around three continents, and just when you are upside down and crying for mercy, you swerve off to a different place, moved by characters rarely written about in Irish fiction. Brilliantly written with a natural ear for dialogue and a deep love for those unrooted headcases who wander the globe open to adventure. From the dark institutions of Ireland they take on the world and grab life bare handed, as if it were the throat of a cobra slithering into your jail cell.
—Emer Martin, author of *Thirsty Ghosts*

Montague writes with a direct, visceral poetry and this whole collection is the work of a born storyteller.
—Mike McCormack, author of *Solar Bones*

Conor Montague writes neon draped prose, characters caught, lost, or living entranced in a smelter of realities. His words conjure a misfit's vision, a child's delight, a killer's desperate play-land. Akin to Henry Miller, Conor Montague writes of 'lost souls downtown' and the constant lurking yearn for lives other than our own.
—Órfhlaith Foyle, author of *Three Houses in Rome*

The characters in *Capital Vices* are tightly wound and on edge in Montague's intense visceral dramas. Montague has the ear of a dramatist – acute to the darkly funny sounds of people trying to talk their way out of trouble. Both lyrical and absurd, Montague's stories are a joy to read.
—Martina Evans, author of *American Mules*

With *Capital Vices* Montague has created a memorable cast of characters; errant, wayward, misplaced, and all the time scavenging for their place in the scheme of things. A collection replete with whiskey wisdom; ache and edge; heart and humour; vigour and poignancy, the swish and bluster of life.
—Alan McMonagle, author of *Laura Cassidy's Walk of Fame*

A roller coaster ride through time, from Ireland to India with a stopover in Disney World. Montague's stories are packed to the brim with craic and cringe in equal measure. Written in technicolour, an ensemble cast of characters are all tested to the limit with unexpected results. This magical blend of flash fiction and short stories is fresh and inventive, I laughed out loud and cried in turn.
—Aoibheann McCann, author of *Marina*

CAPITAL VICES

Conor Montague is from Galway. Prior to settling on a pen as his weapon of choice, Conor winged it as a nightclub manager, bin man, music promoter, builder, adventure travel guide, academic, bare-knuckle boxer, dive master, estate agent, marijuana grower, tutor coordinator, magazine editor, sports coach, security consultant, researcher, stand-up comic and DJ, spending time in East Africa, North Africa, Southeast Asia, India, Nepal, South America, the Caribbean, Australia, the US and mainland Europe.

Conor is a graduate of the MA in Writing at NUI Galway. He is co-director of London Writers Eclective and resident playwright at the Irish Cultural Centre, Hammersmith.

His short fiction has been placed/shortlisted for The Bridport Prize, the Hammond House International Literary Prize, The V.S. Pritchett Short Story Prize, The Bath Flash Fiction Award, Reflex Flash Fiction Competition, Writer's Bureau Short Story Prize, the Fish Prize and Flash 500.

Conor also writes for stage and screen.

Capital Vices

Conor Montague

Aideen,

Thanks for all of your support and your splendid company over many years.

Now we just sit back...

REFLEX PRESS

First published in 2023 by Reflex Press
Abingdon, Oxfordshire, OX14 3SY
www.reflex.press

A CIP catalogue record of this book is
available from the British Library.

ISBN: 978-1-914114-01-4

1 3 5 7 9 10 8 6 4 2

Printed and bound in Great Britain by
Severn Print, Gloucestershire.

Cover image by Bad Dog
www.baddog.ie

www.reflex.press/capital-vices/

For my mother, Chris Montague, who lived in constant fear of me publishing a book and died without once discouraging it.

A capital vice is that which has an exceedingly desirable end so that in his desire for it, a man goes on to the commission of many sins...

—St. Thomas Aquinas

CONTENTS

Kindle

He doesn't turn, remains stooped into fireplace, resurrecting embers.

'How much does that pay?'

'Not much at first.'

Stubs of fingers coax twigs and shavings, singed sap the perfume of days together chopping. I hand him a clod of turf. He looks at it, turns it in his hand, drops it back into the basket and chooses one long and curved. It arches over the centre of the smouldering mound.

'And later?'

'Hard to know. Depends.'

He selects three short, straight pieces, leans them side by side against the long, curved clod, then repeats the process on the other side. Sinks onto haunches and whips off his tweed flat cap, retrieves a nipped Woodbine from behind the peak. Grabs a twig as it flares, sparks up the nipper. Acrid tobacco, sweet resin, earthy turf, scents of childhood, of manhood, of home. He exhales into the fireplace.

'That's a great word... Depends.'

Another pull. Another exhale. The fire catches, engulfing the arch. I place a couple of sods upon the flames. Bog bristles crackle. He shifts up onto the armchair, flicks ash onto the hearth before crossing his legs.

'You won't take the farm?'

'It's not what I want.'

'Good work.'

'I know.'

Two deep pulls. He flicks the butt into the fire and rises.

'You'll have a sup a tae?'

'I will.'

He plucks two mugs from the dresser, pours treacle tea, dribbles milk in that precise way of his. I add another sod as he turns.

'It's no different from working the bog, Pops.'

'How'd you make that out?'

'The digging, the spreading, the footing, the harvest.'

'Will it keep you warm?'

'Different kind of warmth.'

He passes a steaming mug.

'Will you promise me one thing?'

'I will.'

'Promise you won't turn out like that bollocks, Yeats.'

The Bat Man of Hat Salat

We were at Pong's kicked back in hammocks when Radish burst screaming from his beach hut with balls ablaze. He flailed across the scorching sand like a concussed gnat, his Mohican a neon green fin slicing through muggy air to plunge into the sea. He surfaced as a thunderclap blasted a bolt of lightning onto the exposed reef twenty metres offshore. The bay flashed, as did Radish, briefly brilliant before he slumped into the water. Raindrops big as marbles sluiced from contrary clouds, their clatter off coconut palms routing the evening's frog cacophony.

Two bikini-clad Swedish women, recent arrivals to the beach, dropped snorkel gear and sprinted through the deluge to where Radish bobbed face-down and naked. Pong stopped his mulching of weed, dropped his Gurkha knife, swung down from his elevated bamboo platform, and loped to the water's edge. He glanced skyward, darted into the water, and dragged Radish up onto the beach. Charlie shifted in his hammock.

'Those shrooms fairly kicked in.'

'I'm pretty sure that really happened.'

Charlie squinted through the rain for a moment before speaking.

'If Radish is dead, that's one hell of an exit.'

'Best exit ever.'

'Is Heidi kissing him?'

'Performing CPR. She's not Swiss. She's Swedish. Both of them are.'

'I know. I was chatting to them earlier.'

'Why'd you call her Heidi?'

'That's her name.'

'Fair enough.'

Adrenaline surged from my gut, tingled along nerve fibres, jellified legs. I shuddered back into my hammock. No way me or Charlie would be moving any time soon. Heidi would have to deal with Radish. I retrieved binoculars from my lap, peered towards where Radish lay unresponsive beneath Heidi's puckered lips. A rabble of backpackers, package tourists and locals blossomed around the scene. Heidi's companion began chest compressions, furious sets between kisses. Radish remained unresponsive; limbs splayed into raging rivulets flushing through the sand. A hunched, bare-chested figure lurched into my bicircular view, swept the two Swedes aside and straddled Radish.

'Hey Charlie, who's this mad bastard? Jesus, it's you.'

Charlie punched Radish in the chest, punched him again and again, roared at the prone figure, a wild feral roar that challenged the apocalyptic thunder and rose above the white noise of the rain. A Thai woman screamed at him to stop. The two Essex boys staying at Green Papaya attempted to drag him from his perch. Charlie nutted one, hoisted the second into the sea, resumed his crazed assault. Three thumps and Radish arced upwards, spewed a spout of water, inhaled.

Charlie flipped Radish onto his side, stood, staggered back towards the bar slick with sweat and rain. He tumbled onto his back, rolled over, crawled the final stretch and ascended the steps. He used Pong's platform to pull himself to his feet, leant upon it a moment to catch breath, lurched sand-streaked and wild-eyed across the bar to flop into his hammock. He wrapped the canvas around his body and turned his battle-worn face towards me. I could see into every pore, into every scar, sink into the deep black ponds of his pupils.

'What's with the binoculars?'

'Binoculars?'

'I'm beside you, fuckwit.'

I coaxed the binoculars from my eyes, considered them in my hands, stroked the twin barrels, looked to Charlie. His soaked glower appeared disembodied, ghostly in the cantankerous flashes, as if his head had been severed and placed high upon his hammock as a warning to others. Heidi and her friend heaved a naked Radish up the steps, aided by the lad Charlie flung into the sea, a gangly wide boy with pierced eyebrows and Union Jack shorts. His stocky companion followed, clutching the bloody mush of his nose, crossed hammers tattoo on a chunky bicep. He glared at Charlie through sunken eyes as he passed. Heidi lowered Radish onto a mat and placed an axe-cushion behind his neck. The rabble chattered into the bar. Spliffs passed through the group as all pondered the same question. How did Radish manage to set his balls ablaze?

Radish gaped up at their faces, sprawled with genitals singed black, flaccid penis blistered, Mohican a drenched green mop draped across shaven dome. His normally crimson face had faded porcelain white, expression that of an abductee about to be probed by aliens. Strings of kelp clung to his scrawny inked torso, their iodine reek languishing in the charged air, contributing a tart tang to the sweet marijuana smoke billowed beneath the bar's thatch canopy.

Achara's slender figure bustled from behind the bar bearing blankets, pursued by yapping children who squirmed through bodies to point and screech at the freak catch laid out upon the floor. She swept her clutch aside, emptied a bottle of coconut oil onto Radish's genitals, threw a blanket over him and handed one to each of the Swedish women. She motioned to Radish to rub the oil slow and easy into his skin before ushering her cackle of children back behind the bar and into the house. Heidi looked to where Pong rummaged around his bamboo platform.

'Have you called an ambulance?'

Pong stopped his searching, grinned his black-toothed grin, gestured towards the rain.

'No roads. It is impossible.'

Heidi pulled her blanket tight around her shoulders and strode across the room to stand before Charlie's head. A ruby nose stud flashed red with a flick of damp ringlets before she spoke.

'You did well.'

'It's what I do. I save lives.'

Heidi smirked down at Charlie.

'You're tripping.'

'I'm tripping.'

She eased down into an adjacent hammock, eyes on the room. Deranged debate swirled around Radish. Ari Kiwi, a one-eyed Māori staying in the hut next to ours, suggested Radish may have been lighting his farts. He had a friend who set curtains ablaze in a hostel in Cusco. Charlie boomed beside me.

'Leave him alone, to fuck.'

All turned to face us, their features so vivid, I flapped grasping hands in front of my face to check I wasn't looking through binoculars. 'Binocular's' I shouted, as if that single word was adequate explanation for my wild gesturing. Baffled expressions honed-in on me. Perhaps if I showed everybody the binoculars, it would clear up any misunderstanding. I felt around my hammock, was unable to find them, swung to one side and looked onto the floor. No sign of binoculars, but I had become entangled in my hammock, face down with arms pinned to my side by the tightened canvas. I remained still, not wishing to draw further attention to myself by struggling or calling for help. A troop of black ants marched by beneath, long antennae swirling like horsewhips, no doubt in excitement at spotting a gigantic grub suspended above. It would be a matter of time before they gathered their forces and attacked.

I felt a weight on my back and screamed, certain a ravenous wolf spider had dropped from the ceiling. I was spun upright. The single eye of Ari Kiwi looked down at me.

'You alright, mate?'

He turned to Charlie's disembodied head.

'Sorry, Charlie, didn't think.'

The rabble dispersed to mats and cushions scattered about the bar. Akara placed extra candles about the room, distributed Chang and Mekong, served food, cleared empties, plonked the house bong onto the table by Ari Kiwi, shot dagger eyes at an oblivious Pong, who was again rummaging around his platform. The bar gradually settled into the soft rhythm of the pounding rain. I drifted into a stupor, the cool, moist air silk upon my face, stoned burble of our fellow travellers a lullaby, blend of salt, spices and weed an aromatic pillow.

'You fucking broke my nose, mate. You know that?'

The jagged tone hacked through my reverie. Two Essex boys at the foot of our hammocks, glaring at Charlie. The stocky one was swelled and blackened around his eyes. Blood trickled onto a soaked singlet from nostrils plugged with paper napkins. He gripped a pint bottle in a right hand with WEST tattooed across its knuckles. No response from Charlie, faced straight ahead, body cocooned in hammock.

'You fucking hear me or what?'

Charlie's head rolled. Their eyes locked. Tension oozed through the bar, smothered chatter. Gangly Wide-Boy sized me up through deranged eyes, vein throbbing through left temple, pint glass tight to his hip. The downpour stopped as abruptly as it had begun.

The instant silence threw the Essex boys. They froze, like am-dram actors struck with stage-fright. A loud, prolonged groan from Radish, his first utterance since slumping into the sea. Heidi rose from her hammock and knelt beside him. Another loud, prolonged groan. The Essex boys turned towards Radish, who had cast off his blanket to writhe naked on the floor. Attempts to lean forward and inspect his blistered balls brought anguished squawks, setting his oiled genitalia flapping. The Essex boys looked at one another and scooted from the bar, almost running up the beach in their haste to be away from this insanity.

Heidi's friend joined her, a squat blonde with a gecko tattooed onto her left calf. Together they eased Radish's shoulders to the floor. Heidi propped him up on a cushion. Her friend opened the bottle in her hand and poured more coconut oil onto Radish's crotch. Leaving the bottle to one side, she dropped her hand and began to massage the oil soft and slow into his balls. Radish's long face contorted with conflicting expressions. Charlie sat up slightly, leant forward.

'Heidi.'

Heidi walked to Charlie's disembodied head. Sand-sprinkled lips scrunched as he hacked and spat words.

'Ribs... Bust... Painkiller... Strong... Painkiller.'

'His ribs. Of course. You cracked his ribs.'

Heidi turned to her friend.

'Rachel, have you any painkillers?'

'I have co-codamol.'

'No.'

Charlie didn't concur with that treatment plan. He shaped for another scrunched delivery.

'Pong... Tell Pong.'

A fruit bat swooped beneath the canopy as Heidi crossed the room. It circled Charlie, a crazed clockwork mobile above his canvas cot, slipped out into the night when a bleary-eyed Pong shuffled over.

'Pong... Sally... Get Sally.'

'For you, Charlie? It is late, no.'

'Friend... My friend... Sally for my friend... You can do, yes?'

Pong looked down to where Radish squirmed through his balls rub.

'I can do.'

Charlie's hammock cocoon split open to reveal Pong's Gurkha knife resting easy in his right hand. He passed it hilt first. Pong smiled, bowed as he accepted the knife.

'I think I lose.' He pointed to his platform. 'I think I leave there but gone. I get Sally, yes.'

Pong's teenage daughter entered the bar and lay down next to Radish. She positioned a cushion beneath her elbow and placed the lip of a long-stemmed pipe into his mouth. Radish gazed into her eyes as she held a black nugget over a candle flame and coaxed a bubbling tarlike substance into the pipe's narrow bowl. He inhaled on her nod, winced at the chest expansion. The wincing stopped at the third hit. He lay back after the fifth and closed his eyes.

The incense aroma of the opium lent a sacred ambiance to Pong's pokey beach bar, all of us worshippers at this temple of the absurd, this temple where the sick could heal, and men could be slain for a moment of poor judgement. Relentless visions when I closed my eyes. A hand with WEST tattooed across the knuckles attempts to prevent a mess of intestines spilling from a slashed gut. Rich, slick blood cascading onto Radish. The Swedish women scream as Charlie slices the jugular of Gangly Wide-Boy. Blood sprays across the room to splash onto Pong's smile. 'My knife. You found my knife.'

It was afternoon when I came to. A mud-splattered songthaew had arrived to pick up Radish. Rachel and the driver took an arm each and manoeuvred his Kubla Khaned figure from the bar. Radish's orange shorts had been retrieved from his hut, and a crimson hue had seeped back into his blissed face. I lay listening to Heidi recount the night's events to Vince and Ciara, a Canadian couple who had arrived at the beach the previous afternoon only to be confined to their hut by the storm. Radish would be transported to the hospital at Thong Sala, and Rachel, who worked as a nurse in Stockholm, would accompany him. Vince let out a low whistle, fingered a scraggy blonde beard.

'Sounds like quite the kerfuffle.'

'Quite the kerfuffle,' agreed Ciara, a lithe dreadlocked woman with curious eyes and a voice like warm milk, 'our kind of place.'

A kerfuffle? Their kind of place? I hoped they didn't expect this level of entertainment every night. Ciara leaned into Heidi.

'How did Radish set his balls ablaze?'

Before Heidi could respond, Vince whistled his low whistle and pointed across the bar.

'Who's that guy? Who's Batman?'

Charlie sat cross-legged and motionless on Pong's bamboo platform. His left elbow rested on the timber outer railing; peeled banana perched snug in his raised hand. A large fruit bat fluttered at the banana, nibbling the flesh, its snout inches from Charlie's, its face equally frightful. The three stood transfixed by man and bat for a few moments before Heidi answered.

'That's Charlie. Charlie saves lives.'

The Integrity of Cockroaches

Our bus swung through a ragtag of scrawny children and belched to a halt. Men, women, boys, girls, dogs, chickens, two black pot-bellied pigs, and a sadhu jostled screamed climbed pushed and clawed their way out onto rust-coloured dirt to a thunderous staccato of firecrackers. JD, jolted from his slumber, screamed and dived to the floor, positive we were under attack from Kalashnikov-bearing radicals. After a few moments flat on the filthy surface, he turned a smudged face towards me.

'Where are we?'

'Gorakhpur.'

'Why are we stopped?'

'Must be stopped for the night?'

He climbed to his feet, brushing dust from filthy combat shorts.

'Fuck me, it's hot. Where's everyone gone?'

He squinted into the bustle as if the answers were spelt out in the strings of fairy lights spread over the town like an enchanted web. The driver pointed towards us as he shouted through the door. JD drew his *Lonely Planet* guide from its low-slung holster on his right leg.

'I'll suss it out.'

He walked to the driver, and an animated conversation ensued, JD pointing at his opened guide and the driver gesticulating to relate the external world to the alien words JD threw at him. Two teenage wisps ascended the steps to join the discussion, followed by a skittle-shaped middle-aged man in a sequined shirt. The older man had a few words of English and pointed from book to town with calm assurance as his three companions babbled over one another. JD returned.

'We're in Gorakhpur. Stopped until morning. Too late to travel further, border closes at night or something.'

'That crash cost us.'

'We're leaving for Sunali at five. About three hours from here.'

I lifted my rucksack and swung it over my shoulder.

'Better find a bed, I suppose.'

'The Standard is just over there. Best hotel in the area.'

A cackle of shysters descended as we disembarked, all exclusive agents for 'very clean, very nice' hotels. JD pointed to a silhouette set back from the road about fifty metres away. It came into focus through the half-light as we gradually shook ourselves free of touts. Paint peeled from pocked walls in long strips to reveal plaster that crumbled into a stagnant open drain along the front wall. The Standard Hotel looked like it had sustained cannon fire in its recent past. JD held his guide before him like a divining device. Sweat streamed down his high forehead, smearing the smudge along his right cheekbone.

'Best hotel in the area?'

'Apparently so.'

'Looks like they neglected to include the 'sub' prefix.'

'The *Lonely Planet* recommends it.'

'Let me see.'

I stood baking beneath the weak amber glow of the area's sole streetlight. It pulsated as I read.

If you're catching the 5a.m. bus to Sunali (at the border), then the hotels opposite the railway station are most convenient, but they're certainly nothing special, and this area is very noisy. The Hotel Raj has appealing single/doubles with attached bathrooms for Rs 60/100. The Hotel Gupta & Tourist Lodge is no better and has rooms with common bath for Rs 50/80 or Rs 70/100 with attached bath. Much better is the Standard Hotel (TEL: 33-6439), with singles/doubles with attached bathrooms for Rs 70/125, and they've got the mosquito problem under control with netting on the windows.

We looked through the Diwali celebrations to our dilapidated dirt-caked bus. A firework screeched by our faces as we turned back towards the hotel.

'Looks a shithole.'

JD snatched his guide and waved it in an arc towards the town.

'They're all shitholes. Please. I can't traipse around in this heat.'

'Suppose it is near the station.'

'A station we have to leave at five a.m. Let's not complicate things. It'll be grand for a few hours.'

'I need a shower if nothing else.'

A mottled goat arched its back and sprayed the front step with chocolate-coloured pellets as we approached. The manager was even less welcoming, though it was reasonably early, and a carnival was in full swing outside his door. Dressed in a sweat-soaked turquoise shirt, he stood behind a battle-scarred mahogany counter beneath a thousand-watt light bulb around which was gathered the largest swarm of mosquitoes we'd ever seen. When the *Lonely Planet* asserted the Standard Hotel had got the mosquito problem under control, they obviously meant they managed to gather them all together in one building. The place smelt of festering sewage-marinated laundry.

'You want room?'

More challenge than question. He placed fists upon counter and glared from beneath a thick mono-brow.

'How much?'

'One hundred fifty Rupee.'

'Can we see?'

'One hundred fifty Rupee.'

'We give you one hundred Rupee.'

'One hundred fifty Rupee.'

'You're quite the negotiator.'

'One hundred fifty Rupee.'

He slammed two registration forms on the mahogany. One hundred fifty Rupee it was. As we tackled inane questionnaires, mosquitoes fell onto our heads and down our necks and onto the counter like black sleet. They were hitting the red-hot bulb and incinerating. We swept them off our respective forms as we wrote. Having filled in his paternal grandmother's maiden name, JD asked if there was food available.

'Kitchen is closed.'

'What about outside?'

The manager shrugged his shoulders and bobbed his head, which translated into 'either give me baksheesh or go find your own damn restaurant'. We placed cash for the room on the counter and handed him our completed forms. He examined them while we waited, looking from the forms to our faces and back again like an HR manager who suspects he's been handed a forged doctor's cert.

'Passports.'

We placed passports on the counter. He meticulously crosschecked the details with those on the registration forms then copied the same details onto a notepad with a pencil stub no longer than his squared thumbnail. Feeling the pinch of a mosquito, I slapped the side of my neck, which caused him to look up from his task. He closed the notebook, gathered the forms, stowed them beneath the counter, pushed passports towards us, and pointed down the hallway.

'Your room down there, room nine.'

He handed us a gigantic chunk of wood with a small silver key chained to it, presumably in case we were to fall into a fast-flowing river on our way to bed. We knew better than to accept a ground-floor room in the vortex of the great mosquito empire, but thirteen hours broiling in a cramped bus, followed by the registration inquisition, had crashed our brains. We started down a grim grey hallway, lit by two naked florescent tubes, each enclosed in a mesh cage.

'Pretty dodgy area when people feel the need to secure their light bulbs.'

'He seems the paranoid type.'

Two skateboard-sized cockroaches raced out of a doorway on our right and scuttled down the hallway ahead of us. Had we been quick enough we could have leapt on their backs and saved ourselves a walk. The room from which they exited was a kitchen, in the loosest possible sense of the word, and it was obvious our friends had left a major cockroach convention. JD chuckled and put on his Indian accent.

'Kitchen is closed.'

The sound of countless cockroach feet clicking on bare concrete reverberated through the corridor, rising in intensity as we walked deeper into the cesspit.

'I feel like we're in an eighties horror movie.'

'We should split up.'

'You go check out the pet cemetery.'

The two roaches took a sharp right and disappeared under a door.

'Bet that's our room?'

Sure enough, it was room nine. We opened the door, JD holding the timber block while I turned the key. I flicked a switch to illuminate a hectic floor. Cockroaches of various sizes, at least thirty of them, ran in all directions. Energised by their panic, we went to town on these glitches in God's great plan. We winced at the crunches beneath our boots at first but eventually worked ourselves into frenzy, shouting as we performed a surreal jig around a room that would make a cell in the Bangkok Hilton positively desirable.

'Take that, you filthy fuck!'

'Not quite fast enough.'

'Die you piece of shit.'

Soon the floor was littered with bodies. A lone survivor escaped through a gash in the external wall a Jack Russell could have comfortably run through. I stopped JD as he began to sweep the dead to one side with his foot.

'Leave them! As a warning to the rest.'

'I'll plug up the wall.'

JD rummaged for old newspaper and other filler while I inspected the en suite facilities. The customary concrete cubicle boasted a sunken floor-hole which pulsated with six-legged trespassers. A rusted showerhead hung precariously from a single nail high on the wall, and a brass tap wept into a yellow plastic bucket, which was itself adjacent to an opening that rendered JD's labours in the next room pointless. If a Jack Russell could have run through the opening in the bedroom wall, then a fully-grown Labrador could have romped through this one to splash into the fermenting pool of filth on the other side. I returned to the bedroom, grabbed the makings, and skinned up. Two metal beds were the only furnishings, prison-style, with flimsy foam mattresses crowned by ragged, stained mosquito nets. JD scraped his bed closer so we could pass the spliff without stretching. We lay smoking on blood-flecked sheets.

'Those two ran down to warn the rest, you know.'

'Looked like it alright.'

'They could hear us booking in. Cockroaches have great hearing, you know, probably listening from inside the door of the kitchen.'

'Think it's great smell they have.'

'That as well, but they also have great hearing.'

'JD. I doubt they understand English.'

JD reflected on what I'd said a moment. He imitated our gracious host.

'Kitchen is closed. Kitchen is closed.'

'I'm starved. Haven't eaten all day.'

'We'd those bananas.'

'Jesus, when was that?'

'About midday.'

'Ten hours. We're due a snack.'

'Should have a mooch if nothing else.'

'A quick look. I'm wrecked. How long were we on that piece-of-shit bus?'

'Too long. C'mon, get it together.'

We took turns under the shower's tepid dribble, an attempt to freshen up and wash at least some of the thick red grime from our bodies. We left the light on, so our enemies would see their dead and think twice about fucking with us, carried our chunk of wood down to the manager. He looked at us as if we had just flung steaming dog shit onto the counter, snatched the key and walked into his back office without a word.

Gorakhpur took Diwali seriously. Children threw firecrackers and waved sparklers, men shouted and gesticulated, women in flowing effervescent robes balanced baskets of spices on heads as they browsed, and horns beeped incessantly. Fairy lights and flaming torches lit the scene. Varied scents clung to us as we walked: jasmine, chai, frying vegetables, raw sewage, charred meat, cow dung, perfumes, stagnant water, sandalwood incense, and a couple I couldn't identify. All blended into a cocktail only the adventurous would sample by choice. We paused at a stall where a teenage boy fried samosas. They didn't look the best but were an option if we didn't find anything better. Boiling oil would have hopefully killed whatever microorganisms had already made their home in the batter. As we crossed the main street, we were almost trampled by an elephant dressed in the gaudy sequined garb of Rajasthan. A turbaned mahout screamed abuse from his elevated perch, waving a hooked stick over his head by way of emphasis. JD was shaken by the near miss.

'You know that's the first vehicle we've come across that hasn't been blowing its horn... Only because it doesn't have one, of course.'

'I wouldn't be so sure.'

JD looked to the reason for the elephant's restlessness. A hot female obviously lurked within smelling distance. We edged our way through the bustle, scanning for decent food. Stalls sold a variety of Indian delicacies, all of which were being devoured before our eyes by heavy black flies. Vendors brushed them off their wares nonchalantly as we approached, in the manner of French pâtissiers brushing excess icing sugar from prize éclairs. After half an hour of pushing through the melee, JD stopped a cycle rickshaw, upon which sat a wizened, skeletal man who looked to be about two hundred years old. JD mimed eating as he imparted instructions, speaking slowly and deliberately, leaving no syllable unstressed.

'We are look-ing for food! Do you know a res-taur-ant?'

The man weighed us up, in the physical rather than metaphorical sense of the term.

He nodded a tiny prune head.

'Yes.'

'You are sure... A res-taur-ant?'

He assessed each of us again, cowering as JD leaned closer. Had he a tail it would have been tucked firmly between his legs. He was obviously lower caste and had exceeded the life expectancy of his kind. To judge by his demeanour, he didn't consider this a good thing.

'Yes.'

We climbed aboard the rickshaw. Our driver looked even scrawnier from behind, a condition emphasised by how difficult he found it to get the vehicle moving. He pushed with two feet on the right-hand pedal, simultaneously pulling on the handlebars. Huge rasping gasps were his only reward. He rested briefly, head bowed, then tried again. JD offered to get off but had a rant thrown back at him in a familiar voice.

'Fuck's sake, it's Grandpa Simpson.'

The tragedy of the ludicrous scene was lightened by this most Western of voices, and we giggled as he raged at the pedal and overweight Westerners and life in general. I decided to cut our losses before he dropped dead.

'C'mon, we'll grab another one.'

'Give him a chance. He'll be fine once he gets going.'

Sure enough, on the next attempt, he managed to push the pedal downwards, and we rolled slowly forward, two Caesars on a chariot powered by a throwback to the days when one could work a slave to death with no qualms of conscience. He jumped from pedal to pedal to keep our momentum going. Three scrawny cows ambled past on the right, and a group of children pointed and waved as they skipped alongside on the left. The road took a slight downward trajectory, and we sped up slightly, slowly leaving children, cows and town in our wake. JD was concerned at leaving town. Surely that would be the most logical location for a restaurant. He tapped a shoulder blade.

'We go to res-taur-ant, yes?'

'Yes.'

The driver pointed ahead and again ranted in his indecipherable Grandpa Simpson voice, giving out to us for not trusting him. We came to a T-junction and turned left down a puckered tarmac road. Cars and trucks zoomed past, far too close. The lack of street lighting left us invisible to all but the most observant of drivers. Our guide moaned from the effort, laboured dry heaves that sounded increasingly like a death rattle. Still he pedalled, resigned to the constant toil and suffering that was his lot in life. In a culture with so many deities, it would be difficult to apportion blame to any one God.

Just when it seemed he was about to drop dead, we pulled up to a grand looking house, which upon closer inspection proved to be a small hotel. There was no sign of activity. If there was a restaurant within, it was a closely guarded secret. I took over speaking duties.

'My friend, where is the restaurant?'

'Yes,' he said, pointing at the building.

I rang the bell in the hope that our guide was better informed than he appeared. No response. I walked around the side of the building. There were well-kept gardens and all the appearances of a middle-class establishment. I returned to JD and our driver having a heated discussion.

'He wants a hundred and fifty Rupee.'

The old man's black eyes sparkled, a toothless smile an attempt to soften the blow. No cycle rickshaw costs more than ten Rupee, perhaps twenty for a long journey. One hundred and fifty Rupees was taking the piss, despite the undoubted hardship endured in getting us to this mystery location. I spoke slowly.

'One hundred and fifty too much. We no pay.'

'Yes.'

He bowed, surrendering to my sense of decency. I realised that 'yes' was the only word of English our friend possessed, and he answered it to everything.

'I give you fifty Rupee and you bring back.'

No response. Humidity increased each second. We were drenched in sweat, beacons to every malarial mosquito within a ten-mile radius. Exhausted, starving, and a long way from our hotel, arguing with an eighty-year-old Indian with one word of English who may or may not have the physical reserves to get us back into town.

A red sports car with tinted windows pulled into the driveway, and two plump men emerged from the air-conditioned interior. They were dressed in tailored silk suits, beige and lilac respectively, garnished with flash ties and gold cufflinks. The driver approached through a haze of citric cologne.

'What is going on here?'

He seemed friendly, so I explained the situation: that we were looking for a restaurant and got a rickshaw to this location.

'Restaurant is closed, very late.'

'Yes, so we gathered.'

'What he try to charge?'

'He wants a hundred and fifty Rupee.'

'From Gorakhpur?'

'Yes, we were looking for a place to eat. I'll give him fifty Rupee.'

He glared at me.

'Fifty Rupee! You give him ten Rupee, no more. I will do.'

He took a coin from his pocket and walked to the old man, who stood by his rickshaw with head bowed. He pushed the coin into his right hand and unleashed a verbal barrage in Hindi. The old man retorted, obviously trying to explain that he had almost died carrying two overweight Irishmen through stifling heat for miles, and surely deserved more than ten Rupees. I was inclined to agree, but before I could interject, the man smacked our driver across the face and sent him tumbling into his rickshaw, which he grabbed to hold himself upright. He attempted to turn his vehicle around so he could make his escape. The other gentleman availed of the opportunity to dish out a clip across the ear, like an Irish schoolmaster back in the good old days, drove the poor fellow back in the other direction. Our guide ranted as he faced the rickshaw towards the road and attempted to mount. A kick up the arse from the driver sent him flying up over the saddle. He banged his chest off the handlebars and bounced back onto the crossbar, from where he slid back up onto the seat. He pedalled as fast as his spindly legs could push; his long, anguished cry gradually swallowed by the night.

The two men, having completed their good deed, bid us goodnight and walked into the hotel, closing the door after them. We stood gob-smacked for a moment before JD announced the need for a taxi and walked to the side of the road as if we had just exited a bar in downtown Manhattan.

'Forget about it. We're walking.'

'You never know, worth a try.'

'Can you believe those two fucks?'

JD glanced at me.

'It's nothing to do with us. C'mon, we'll start walking so.'

'It is to do with us. That wasn't fucking on.'

JD placed his hands on my shoulders.

'Listen, those guys could be chiefs of police for all we know, we have to let it go.'

He was right. We turned and began to plod through the blackness. With each heavy step, our guilt deepened. Though the old man had tried to pull a fast one and had dropped us at a closed restaurant in the middle of nowhere, we had become fond of him. Ten Rupee was an insult. To judge by his rasping lungs and malnourished physique, possibly the final insult.

Thirty-five long hot minutes later, we reached town, dreaming of greasy fried samosas. Silence and darkness stood together in greeting, punctuated by rats scavenging for scraps among sleeping cows, people and dogs. So great was the contrast from the town we had left just over an hour before, I got the shivers, half believing an apocalyptic event had taken place after we'd been ferried to safety by the most unlikely guardian angel in history. Samosas were off the menu.

The bars across the doorway of the hotel were locked. I rattled them loudly to awaken whatever security slumbered within. A paunchy guard materialised from the darkness. He slowly swung open the bars and handed us our chunk of wood without a word. We entered our room to discover the light had been turned off, no doubt by Gorakhpur's homegrown version of Basil Fawlty. I flicked the switch. Something was different. We stood exhausted, attempting to solve the puzzle. I spotted slight movement on the floor, and realisation hit.

'There's more of them.'

'What?'

'Cockroaches. There's twice as many bodies.'

We walked into the room, and cockroaches, motionless until then, scattered in all directions from the bodies of fallen comrades. We dredged up energy for a final frenzy, this time visualising different Indian characters as we crunched vile vermin. There was Basil Fawlty, and the two rich fucks with bad attitude, and the cheery security guard, and the lazy little shitbag who'd closed his samosa stall before we got back into town. All smashed beneath our boots.

We stripped, showered and skinned up a spliff each, so we wouldn't have to reach out under our nets once tucked in. We lay smoking, secure in our cocoons, tepid water our sole refreshment. JD looked at me.

'You know why those cockroaches came back?'

'Shit on our pillows?'

'They're amazing creatures; when we stamp on them, they emit an ultrasonic scream and release an enzyme, so all of the cockroaches around know they're in trouble. That's why they were all gathered around the bodies. Checking for survivors, back to help their mates.'

'Should have smacked those fucks earlier.'

'Jesus, will you let it go. Not our business.'

JD snored as I visualised the hero's welcome the old man would have received from his loved ones had he returned home with a hundred and fifty-Rupee, long-lost manhood restored for one final glorious moment. I had the chance to gift him that moment, to swallow my pride and let him scam me. Obvious how much he needed a break. Three quid. It wouldn't buy a pint back home.

Ant squadrons invaded the space, marching in tight columns from cracks in the blistered plaster. They swarmed over the black carcasses, dismantling them, carrying tiny segments back to base. Before long, there was nothing left but bare husks shivering in the thermal currents rising across the concrete. I dozed and dreamt of the old man. His rigid body on its back by the side of a dark road with limbs pointed skywards. Ants marched from the night to dismantle his frail frame. Bare bones glinted in the morning sun, bronze glow from the ten-Rupee coin clutched in his skeletal fist. Bloated cockroaches climbed from his skull through empty eye-sockets, swallowed the last of his memories as they skulked back into the undergrowth.

Star Cross'd

We traipse in silence through damp fragrant Bloomsbury streets. Magnolia petals strewn about sopping paths glisten like moonlit lilies upon contemplative ponds. 'The mansion of the Earl stood at the far end of the square,' I venture, 'replaced by that grandiose monument to grand larceny.' You can't help but smirk at my feigned outrage, squint towards the north corner as if Southampton House might loom through swirling squall like Prospero's Island. You grasp my hand and lead me onto stepping-stones of patrons and sonnets, dark ladies and platonic love.

Poached eggs and toast in a bright all-night diner. We chat as if there'll be other evenings, long walks into the future, lazy recollections of the past we would share. Sip the pretence with our tea, fortified by its warmth. I tip the sarcastic Irish waiter – gratuity for his walk-on role – and trail your rich cinnamon bouquet into the rain.

Black cab trundles into a pothole, drenches the tartan drainpipes of a screen-swiping hipster. Your giggle gurgles through manic bustle as the hipster spits fire at the heavens. Surge of blind brollies sweep me before a clanging rickshaw. I spring back and parry with matador flourish, strike pose as it clatters past.

I turn to you gone. A bus shoulders its way into traffic. Your silhouette through misted pane evokes the Monet we viewed earlier. Your Gallic lilt introducing *Le Bateau-atelier*. Your absence as you gazed upon the scene. The delicate blush of its mournful sky.

Distilling

You hunker to peer through the fine mesh of the coop. Tangled black ringlets cascade over your pale oval face. Nose scrunches against the sour stench of droppings. You unravel ties which fasten a makeshift trapdoor, swing back the square segment, reach through to grasp a chick. It *cheeps* as you ease it through the opening, cup hand over baffled eyes, lower cheek to yellow down, milk the feel of it on your skin.

Molly raises an eyebrow, limbers to you, rests muzzle on shoulder and sniffs the trembling bird. Siblings clamour over straw in a chaos of *cheeps*. Deeper *clucks* of their mother as she stands with a tremor. You whisper to the brown hen.

'It's alright, Mammy, I'm only saying hello.'

You hold chick to lips, kiss its beak.

'Amn't I? I'm only saying hello.'

'Well, Cáit, is it a boy or a girl?'

You start, swing to face your uncle.

'Patrick, you did it again.'

'I did it again.'

Molly bounds to the tall figure in the doorway, rises with a yelp, plonks paws on black cotton shirt. Patrick cups its head in gnarled hands, scratches ears, allows the dog to lick high cheekbones as he nuzzles her with a wide, dented nose.

'Howya, Molly. Who's the best girl, ha? Who's the best girl?'

He pushes Molly down, nudges a chamber pot aside with his foot.

'I never hear you coming.'

'One of these days, Cáit, one of these days. Mamo has an egg for you inside.'

You return the chick to its family. Patrick crouches, watches the reunion as you refasten ties. Molly nags at Patrick's right elbow.

'Is that your favourite?'

'I don't have a favourite. I love them all.'

You twist the final tie.

'There now, good and tight.'

'Good girl yourself.'

'So the hen won't get out.'

'That's right.'

'And let the fox in.'

'We don't want the fox calling round.'

'Or the weasel.'

'Definitely not the weasel.'

'He'll kill all around him, won't he, Patrick?'

'He will. Throw a bit of breakfast into them there.'

You dart to the table, pluck lid from a stained aluminium pot, grab a handful of meal, return to your uncle's side, dribble fine grain through the mesh. Hen bustles through offspring, sends them tumbling as she scratches and pecks.

'Ah no, I gave her some first. She's not much of a mother.'

Patrick strokes a smudge of turf dust from your cheek with the back of his middle finger. It smells of milk.

'She's a good mother, alright. That'll toughen them up. They won't be in a coop forever, you know.'

He tousles your hair.

'It's a big bad world out there'.

'A big bad world. It's for their own good.'

'Now run in and get breakfast, *Maith an cailín.*'

Smell of turf smoke and baked bread. Your grandmother's slender frame at the range, wellingtons wet from her trek to the spring well, pale legs mud-flecked above the rubber. She ladles an egg from a blackened saucepan onto a chequered tea towel in her left hand.

'How are the chicks?'

'Great, I just gave them breakfast.'

'Good girl yourself, you're lookin' after them well.'

Mamo eases the egg into a wooden eggcup on a side plate at the edge of the range. She places the plate at the head of a long oak table, wipes palms on navy smock, cuts a thick slice of brown bread, drops it onto the plate beside the egg, scoops a knob of butter with the tip of the breadknife and spreads it thick. Purple veins bulge along the backs of her hands, course up sinewy forearms. She retrieves a tired teapot from where it putts at the back of the range.

'Mamo?'

'Yes, loveen.'

'These aren't the same eggs chicks come from?'

'No, loveen, these eggs are for eatin'.'

'It's special eggs the chicks come from.'

'That's right, and 't'is special eggs we'll be havin' tomorrow...'

'Because it's Easter Sunday?'

'Because it's Easter Sunday. And what happened on Easter Sunday?'

'Jesus rose from the dead.'

'That's right, Jesus rose from the dead.'

'It was a miracle wasn't it, Mamo.'

'That's right, a miracle.'

You look to the portrait, tinged red by the perpetual light beneath.

'Mamo?'

'Yes, loveen.'

'Are you afraid of Jesus?'

'Why would anybody be afraid of Jesus?'

'His eyes follow me.'

'Just a trick of the light.'

'Like magic?'

'Not magic. Just your imagination.'

'Are miracles magic?'

'No, loveen, miracles are the work of God. There's no such thing as magic.'

'What about in my stories?'

'They're just pretend.'

You bite into your bread, sup your tea. Mamo grabs a broom, sweeps a sprinkle of turf dust into a small pile by Dev's basket, snatches a square of cardboard from beneath sleeping cat, chokes broom to coax dust onto cardboard.

'Jesus looks sad.'

Mamo flips dust into basket, straightens.

'Wouldn't you be sad if you'd a crown like that?'

'I think I'd be crying, Mamo. It's sticking right into him.'

'He suffered because he loves us.'

'He loves me, doesn't he?'

'He loves all children.'

'Mammy is with Jesus.'

'She is, loveen. Mammy is with Jesus.'

'And Granddad?'

'And Granddad.'

'And Auntie Maureen?'

'And Auntie Maureen.

'I hope they make Jesus happy.'

Mamo rests a hand on your head.

'I know they do, Cáit. Sure they made everyone happy the three of them.'

Patrick enters gripping a wax jacket and small yellow raincoat, drapes both across the back of a chair.

'You're not bringin' the child out in that?'

'In what?'

'It's promised rain again. She'll catch her death.'

'She'll be grand. Haven't I her raincoat there?'

'Fat lot of good it'll be in those showers.'

'I'll be fine, Mamo, won't I, Patrick?'

'You will, bone dry.'

Mamo pours tea, dribbles dregs from the pot.

'There'll be no stayin' bone dry in that rain, I tell ye that for nothin'.'

'We'll go between the showers.'

'Where are we going, Patrick?'

'It's a secret. Only me and the faeries know.'

'Will I see the faeries?'

'You might. If you're watching.'

'Always be watching, isn't that right Patrick?'

'That's right.'

'Will ya stop fillin' the child's head with nonsense.'

Patrick winks at you as Mamo clunks teapot onto range.

'Tea's poured.'

'Thanks, Mamo.'

'Eat up, loveen or it'll be cold on ya.'

A chaffinch whistles its staccato tune from a perch on the freshly trimmed hedge outside the window, blue-pink feathers ruffled from the morning shower. Mamo shifts the large black pot to one side, opens the lid of the range, inserts two stumpy clods, bangs them into the fire with a short black poker. Sparks spiral around her face.

'They're goin' to hang young Manning on Tuesday. T'was on the wireless earlier. Some lad comin' from England to do it.'

'Pierrepoint.'

'What?'

'His name is Pierrepoint. The English hangman. We can't even hang our own.'

'Manning's poor mother I feel sorry for.'

'He deserves no less.'

'What's a hangman, Patrick?'

'The lad that hangs meat for the butchers.'

'So we can look at it?'

'Exactly. So we can look at it.'

Mamo replaces the lid, moves pot back, turns to Patrick, wiping palms on smock.

'Peelers were beyond in Feeney's Wednesday night.'

'So I heard.'

'They get anythin'?'

'No. Paddy Fáda spotted them at the cross and ran back across the land.'

'Have you a run on today?'

'I have. We'll head down to the lake shortly, before the rain comes back.'

You look to your uncle, uneasy.

'Are we going to the shed by the lake?'

'We are.'

Mamo clears your plate, wipes the table.

'Were you there before, Cáit?'

Her eyes upon you as she wipes, you watch the cloth for a moment.

'We were in it yesterday, Mamo. We think there were *Sheógs* there.'

'There's no *Sheógs*. Don't mind that blackguard.'

Mamo whips the tea towel. Patrick blocks it with the back of his hand.

'I didn't say anything to her.'

'He didn't, Mamo, Patrick didn't say anything. We heard them, didn't we, Patrick?'

'We did.'

'What'd you hear?'

'There's an ass-cart in the corner, isn't there Patrick? And it's covered in straw, and we stood beside the straw and we could hear breathing, couldn't we Patrick? And burping.'

'Burpin'?'

'Yes, Mamo, under the straw, and there was a funny smell, like burnt fruitcake. We had to sneak out of the shed, like two shadows. Isn't that right, Patrick?

'That's right, like two shadows.'

Mamo feints with the tea towel as Patrick sups. He flinches, scalds lips.

'I'll give ye shadows. What's on you?'

'What's on you?'

'Frightenin' the child like that.'

'She's not frightened, are you, Cáit?'

'No, Mamo, I'm not frightened. Not when I'm with Patrick, 'cause you'll mind me, won't you, Patrick?'

'I'll mind you.'

'Mind you? He can hardly mind himself. Did ya feed the calves?'

'I did.'

'How's the white-head heifer?'

'She'll be a couple of days yet.'

'She will not be a couple of days. I'll go check on her.'

Mamo flings a cloak over her shoulders, snatches a length of hazel from the corner, mutters out the front door. Patrick drains his tea.

'We'd best get going. Before she comes back and kills the two of us.'

'We'll go while it's dry.'

'That's right. Have you your wellies?'

Into the hallway. Dress for the weather. Patrick fastens your raincoat, ties hood beneath your chin.

'Now. All set.'

'Mamo says there's no such thing as magic.'

'Maybe she's just not watching.'

'Not like us.'

'Exactly, not like us.'

'Always be watching, isn't that right, Patrick?'

'That's right.'

The two of you hand in hand through saturated, garlic-scented laneway. Hazel and alder intertwine above, a green canopy bright in the between-shower glare. Molly bounds walls and plunges through undergrowth with jubilant yelps, arcs of sparkling droplets in her wake. Ruffled water of Lough Corrib. A man smoking by the dilapidated limestone structure set back from the shore.

'Is that Michael Kyne, Patrick?'

'That's the bould Michael Kyne alright. What's wrong?'

'Nothing.'

Patrick stops, turns you to him.

'Do you not like Michael?'

'I do, it's just that...'

'Just what?'

'I'm afraid of him, Patrick.'

'Why would you be afraid of Michael?'

Molly skids into Patrick's hip. You scratch her panting chest, look towards the lake. Patrick's fingers down your cheek, chin cupped in his rough palm. You feel the soft spot in the centre.

'Why are you afraid of Michael?'

'You'll only laugh.'

'I won't laugh, tell me.'

'Promise?'

'I promise.'

'He looks like Mamo's turkey cock... You promised you wouldn't laugh.'

'I'm not laughing.'

'I can see it in your eyes, Patrick.'

'Laughing at Michael I am. It's true for ya, with his tiny eyes and red beak.'

'And the way he walks Patrick.'

You strut around your uncle, elbows flapping, head bobbing. He sinks to his knees, curls onto the soaked ground, laughing, loud as Mamo's jackass. You punch his shoulder. Molly's barks a circle around. Patrick grabs you in his rise. You squeal as the world turns upside down, dizzy when he plonks you on your feet.

'You're a gas woman, Cáit Carter, a gas little woman. 'We'd best get over to Michael. He'll be wondering what we're at.'

'You won't tell him, Patrick?'

'I won't tell him.'

A faint breeze rises off the slate-grey lake, barely enough to ferry the burble of waterfowl from down along the shore. A downpour as you enter the shed. Pelt of raindrops on the galvanised roof. The men smirk.

'I thought you didn't like rain, Patrick.'

'What makes you say that?'

'Didn't you say it to Seamus Bán outside the school the last day?'

'Did I?'

'You did. Seamus said he hadn't been out for a shot in three weeks, and you said 't'was enough to drive a man mad.'

Patrick unfastens your raincoat.

'Sometimes rain is a good thing.'

'It's bad for the hay, isn't it, Patrick.'

'It is. But it's good for other things. There we are. Bone dry.'

'Bone dry. Mamo won't be giving out.'

Michael laughs as he hangs his overcoat from a rusted horseshoe stud stuck high in the rotted doorframe. He spits into his palms, rubs them together.

'You don't want Mamo giving out, I'll tell ye that for nothing.'

The men fork straw down from the cart. You can't hear gurgles or burps, not with the pelting rain, but the shed still smells like burnt fruitcake. Patrick spots you poised by the door, nudges Michael, who turns to you as he hoists down a forkful.

'What age are you now, Cáit?'

'Seven and three-quarters.'

Michael stops forking.

'Is that right? You're a big girl now, isn't she, Pat?'

'She is. All grown up.'

You leave the doorway, edge towards the men. They drag the cart from the corner to reveal two large timber barrels, one smaller barrel, and a bag of turf.

'I remember. I remember.'

'What's that, Cáit?'

'The barrels. They're full of spring water.'

Michael backhands dust from his lapels.

'You hear that, Pat? Spring water, no less. And how do you know that, Cáit?'

''Cause me and Patrick filled them, didn't we, Patrick, a few weeks ago.'

'We did.'

'Fourteen times we went to the well, isn't that right, Patrick?'

'That's right.'

'You hardly drew water, Cáit?'

'I did. I had my two buckets, and Patrick had his two buckets. And we saw the fox at the well, didn't we, Patrick?'

'We did.'

Patrick begins to build a low square structure with flat stones he gathers from along the walls.

'He was lucky you didn't have the gun, Patrick.'

Michael throws on his overcoat, walks into the rain.

'That was one lucky fox, alright.'

Patrick places a handful of straw into the stone structure, adds splinters of the dry wood scattered about the floor. He strikes a match. The straw flares up over the kindling. You join him in feeding the flames.

'Mind your frock doesn't catch fire.'

‘I will, Patrick, ’cause that’s what happened to Auntie Maureen, isn’t it?’

‘That’s right.’

‘Before I was born.’

‘Before you were born.’

Patrick places small black sods of turf upon one another, like a boy building with toy blocks. Michael returns with a large sack over each shoulder, clanks them onto the floor, shakes the water off, sheds overcoat, hangs it back on the stud. He fills his pipe, looking out into the rain. Patrick takes a pot from a sack.

‘That’s as big as Mamo’s pot.’

‘It is.’

‘Is it for boiling water?

‘You’ll see.’

Patrick picks up a dented lid with a large spout, places it beside the pot, reaches into the second sack, grips a curled piece of copper pipe, holds it in front of him, caresses it with right hand, following twists to the end and working back. Flames crackle golden off the copper.

‘What’s that, Patrick?’

‘This is the worm.’

‘The worm?’

‘That’s right.’

‘Like in the ground?’

‘A different kind of worm. A magic worm.’

‘From the faeries?’

‘Exactly, from the faeries.’

‘Did you have to ask them, Michael?’

‘I had to ask King Finnbhear himself. Asking after you, he was.’

‘He was not. Was he, Patrick?’

'I don't know, 't'was Michael talking to him.'

'He was not, Michael.'

'He most certainly was. He gave me this for you.'

A silver three-penny piece bright on Michael's dirt-caked palm. You look to Patrick, take the coin.

'Thank you.'

'Don't thank me. Thank King Finnbhear.'

Michael stoops to gather stones, begins to build another platform to one side of the fire. He looks at you from under his right arm.

'You can buy sweets after mass tomorrow.'

'This is going into my savings, Michael.'

'Savings. Is that so? And what are you saving for?'

'For when I go to America.'

Patrick takes the smaller of the three barrels, hunkers with it between his knees and places the worm inside. You lean on his shoulder as he threads the bottom-end out through a small round hole near the base of the barrel, leaving the top-end flush with the rim. He puts the barrel on the platform Michael built, grabs the large pot, strides to the two remaining barrels and prises open the lid of the first one with the blade of a shovel.

'You're going to leave Wormhole? For America, no less. And when are you going?'

'When I'm finished school, isn't that right, Patrick? I'm going over to see my daddy in New York City.'

'Is that where your daddy is?'

'It is. He works on buildings that are so tall they touch the sky, isn't that right, Patrick?'

Patrick grabs your waist, hoists you over his head.

'Buildings that touch the sky in New York City.'

You settle on his right hip, peer into the opened barrel at a pungent treacle-like substance. It belches its sickly whiff.

'That's not spring water, Patrick.'

'Not anymore.'

'What happened?'

'The *Sheógs* must have got to it.'

'The bad faeries.'

'That's right.'

Patrick dips a chipped mug into the thick liquid, takes a sip, swirls it around in his cheeks, spits it onto the ground. You poke a finger into the mug and taste, scrunch your face.

'You don't like it?'

'It's worse than sloes, Patrick, makes my mouth dry.'

'We'd better change it back into spring water so.'

'How will we do that?'

'We'll have to use magic.'

'Like Aladdin.'

'That's right, just like Aladdin.'

Michael adds a couple of sods to the fire, places the pot on top.

'Aladdin? Is he from around here?'

'No, Michael, he's from far away.'

'Must be from Galway, so.'

'Not Galway, another country, far far away.'

'You tell him, Cáit.'

Patrick eases you to the ground, picks up a bucket, fills the pot with the dark, tangy liquid from the barrel.

'He has a magic lamp.'

'For his bicycle, is it?'

'No, Michael. He doesn't have a bicycle.'

'And how does he get to the village?'

'He has a carpet.'

'A carpet? That won't get him far.'

'It's a flying carpet.'

'A flying carpet? I'll have to buy one of those. What do you think, Pat? Do McDonagh's stock flying carpets?'

'No, Michael. You can't buy them.'

'And where did Aladdin get his? I hope he didn't steal it.'

You pause to consider Michael's flushed face. Patrick hands you a bag.

'Don't mind him, Cáit. Far from flying carpets Michael Kyne was reared.'

'What's that, Patrick?'

'Look and see.'

You let the bag unwind in your grip and look inside.

'Are we going to make bread?'

'Not bread, something else.'

'Does Mamo know we took it?'

' 'T'was her gave it to us.'

'That's alright so. What will I do with it?'

'Give some to Michael there and he'll show you.'

Michael takes a handful. He presses the dough into the space around where the worm exits through the barrel, cups hands to coax it out into a mound which stops just short of the lip.

'Now, Cáit. That's to stop it leaking. If there's any leak, there's no magic.'

You peek into the barrel; empty save the curled copper pipe.

'There's nothing to leak, Michael.'

'No flies on this girl, Pat. We'd best sort that out.'

Michael puts on his overcoat, marches into the rain, bucket in each hand. You watch him fill both buckets from the lake and run back into the shed. He pours water into the barrel containing the worm.

The men wait. Michael smokes his pipe, gazing across the lake from beneath the peak of his tweed flat cap. Patrick remains by the fire. He stirs the pot occasionally, inserts a finger, licks it. You're on the floor beside Molly, kneading a piece of dough, making indents of the three-penny piece, first the face with the hare, then the face with the harp, then both, side by side.

'Grab the head there.'

Michael comes in from the doorway, hands the lid to Patrick, who places it on the pot, guiding the spout over the top end of the worm.

'Have you the bag there, Cáit?'

You run over, hold the bag open for the men. Molly joins the group, sniffs the bag, watches the men seal around the lid, then around where the spout swallows the worm. Patrick hands you a piece. You squish it between fingers, press it around the edges of the lid, feel the pot's warm pulse. Its fruity breath sweetens the bitter turf smoke, reminds you of blackberry jam. Patrick's hand presses on the backs of your fingers.

'Now you have the hang of it, good girl yourself.'

'If it leaks, there's no magic, isn't that right, Patrick?'

'That's right.'

The three of you stoop towards the gurgling pot, heads cocked. Patrick nudges the fire with a charred stick. Michael adds water to the worm barrel, places a jug beneath the worm's mouth. Molly circles and whines, looks at each of you in turn, expectant. Patrick pulls a couple of sods from the fire. Smoke from the smouldering turf stings your eyes. You wipe tears with the hem of your frock. Patrick smiles.

'It's time, Cáit.'

A single puff of steam shoots out of the worm. You pull Patrick's sleeve.

'We'll have a wish each.'

A trickle of clear liquid follows the steam and dribbles into the jug.

'Spring water, Patrick. The magic worked.'

'It did. The magic worked.'

'There is magic. I knew it. I knew it, Patrick.'

Patrick takes the jug, replaces it with a larger one, strides to the doorway and flings its contents onto ferns huddled soaked along a squat stone wall.

'For the faeries.'

An Evening with Bono

Bono is constipated. His back arches. The strain curls lips back over teeth. Jaws spasm. Nostrils shoot twin vapour plumes into the frosty air. It's futile. He peers in at me through the patio door, adopts his forlorn expression. Bastard. He does this on purpose. Well, he can wait. I grab my tea and join Marian in the sitting room.

'How's Bono?'

'The same.'

'You'll have to clean his arse, Adam. He's not coming into the house like that.'

'I know.'

'It's too cold to leave him outside.'

'I know.'

'Who were you on the phone to?'

'Larry. He wants to hook up later.'

'You're not going to the pub again?'

'Won't be long.'

'What's so urgent you have to meet this evening?'

'Said he had to tell me in person. I can ask him to call here.'

'Do not ask him to call here. He'd give a headache to an aspirin, that lad.'

'I'll go to the pub so.'

'You're fierce considerate.'

'Anything to keep you happy.'

'If you want to keep me happy...'

'I know. I know. Clean Bono's arse.'

I return to the kitchen, ignore Bono's face at the window. I rinse my cup and slam it onto the draining board, fill a mop bucket with warm soapy water, stretch rubber gloves onto my hands, grab the bucket and walk out through the patio door to where Bono prances impatiently. Arrogant little bollocks. I ease his ass into the steaming bucket. Orgasmic eye-rolls as I dislodge a black hardened blob and coax brittle debris from the matted hair around his backside. He pushes back into my palm. Low guttural groans as he grinds. I gaze up at the star-stuffed sky, reflect upon what my life has become. Hunkered in the freezing cold gratifying a constipated Bichon Frise. I wish I were Bono.

Killing Donald

I come-to topless, shoeless, and alone, stewing in stench of bleached urine. Ceiling cracks chart the Mississippi delta into a cobwebbed corner. I languish in the bayous, trace routes to Cleveland and New Albany before turning my head. Filth speckles outwards from a steel shitter bolted to a pocked, piss-stained platform. I gasp and groan onto right elbow. Crushing ache between ribs, head throbbing like a throttled airboat. Grey walls spin anticlockwise, stir the scalding dread gurgling deep in my stomach. I flop back onto a thin damp mattress and shut my eyes.

An upright platypus bursts into song. Grotesque head bobs, hatching egg trembles and cracks upon its webbed palm. Painted aborigines leap and whoop around a campfire, flames flickering off poised boomerangs. The rich timbre of didgeridoo melts into jangly Irish trad. Jigging leprechauns throng the starboard bank, angular ginger beards and skewed top hats framing withered faces. I grab Frankie's arm.

'This place is fucked up.'

'It's just the Irish.'

'They don't belong, man. None of them do.'

We drift into lush rainforest. Giraffes leer from above the canopy, baboons bark among fronds. Forest clears to reveal a freak funfair, rainbow carousels and big wheels stuffed with chanting oblong heads. We pass beneath an arch and round a bend. Small people shriek onto the barge.

'The Irish, the Irish are attacking.'

I curl into myself, arms shielding head, brace for a barrage. I peek through fingers to check on Frankie. It's not the Irish. No ginger beards or skewed top hats. These beings are of smooth complexion. A voice bellows from above.

'You gotta get off the ride. You hear me, sir? You need to disembark.'

We stand, sway wide-armed like rookie surfers caught by a sudden swell, unable to muster sufficient courage to leap the six-inch chasm. More small people tumble in from behind, bluster us over the peril. We lurch hand in hand through a narrow tunnel to emerge traumatised into a cotton candy breeze which chills the globules of sweat jewelled across our foreheads. Small people bounce off knees and hips. They're children. The small people are children. Two-headed children. The extra heads bob slightly higher and to one side of their hosts. Their faces look familiar. Where have I seen them before?

Keys jangle. Lock double clicks. A doughy detective with porn star moustache swaggers into the cell, badge clipped onto snakeskin belt. He throws a cotton T-shirt into my face and drops a bottle of water onto the bed.

'Rise and shine. We got work to do.'

I pounce on the water. Drain the bottle.

'What happened?'

He consults a clunky dive watch on his left wrist. Half a thumb is missing.

'That's what we're about to find out, Mr Ryder. That's what we're about to find out.'

'Frankie?'

'Frankie?'

'My friend... Where is he?'

'I'm Detective Frazier...'

A second detective enters. She's lithe and swarthy with cropped raven hair and mirror shades.

'...and this is Detective López. We're the only friends you have in the world right now.'

Frankie's gone. Frankie's gone. Marshmallow legs squish into paving. Arms piston to coax them along, torso uncoupling from trunk as I twitch and gyrate along a brick road past giant twirling teacups. Baloo boogies by, twerks his saggy ass. My nose crunches into the back of a shaven head. I hunker down, face in hands. Frankie stands fixated on Old Glory, unfurled across the night sky by laser beams. Charcoal tendrils from a feast of food stalls distort its stars and stripes. Frankie looks down at me, clutched to his thigh like a randy terrier.

'Dude, either whip it out and start sucking, or get the fuck off my leg.'

He hauls me to my feet, gestures towards the flag.

'Lies, man. Nothing but motherfucking lies.'

Sneezy bobs by, followed by Bashful and Grumpy. I yank Frankie's arm.

'They're dwarves. They're fucking dwarves.'

Frankie scans the crowd.

'They're children, dude. Just children.'

Dopey passes. I poke him by way of demonstration. My index finger sinks into the moist eyeball of a bald child riding the crook of Daddy's arm. Its screech slices through the mayhem. Mom snatches child and holds it close, flings an icy glare towards Dad. Frankie pulls me from a burgeoning cordon of concerned parents, leads me out onto the palace courtyard.

'What did you do that for? It's only a kid.'

'I thought he was Dopey.'

'That's no way to wake him up.'

'No, I thought he was Dopey. The dwarf.'

Frankie looks at me like I've lost all reason and takes off across the courtyard. I fumble after him, wriggling through a flabby kaleidoscope of snarling faces. Everybody knows what I did to the child. A girl with blonde ringlets pokes me with the head of a wand when I jam her head against the hip of a tall, bearded man with a crown of blue neon. Emerge into a formation of faceless soldiers, almost shit myself as they march by on either side, twirling rifles and barking orders. Buzz Lightyear bears down, glint of bloodlust in his drooped eyes. Neurotransmitters and synapses tangle into a tight knot behind my left ear. Spasms flutter through my chest. It's a stroke. I'm having a stroke.

Whiff of liquorice. Frazier and López sit at the other side of a large Formica-topped desk. My distorted face in tandem from the shades of López, sunlight sheer through high window, dust particles disorientated before lethargic fan. Flex dangling from a wall-mounted camera casts a hangman's noose on the wall. Frazier extracts a stick of Orbit from his breast pocket. The crinkle of its slow unwrapping sparks tingles along my spine. He slurps the gum as he sets his pad and picks up a pen. López hits record.

'State your name.'
'Jack Ryder'
'Date of birth?'
'January eighth, 1985.'
'Current address.'
'Downtown.'
'Where downtown?'
'Mai Tai Drive, seventeen seventy-six. Am I under arrest?'
'Should you be?'
'I should have a lawyer present.'
'We're just having a conversation.'
'You know why you're here, Mr Ryder?'
'Frankie.'
'Frankie?'
'Frankie lost the plot.'
Frazier writes and triple underlines 'plot' in his notebook. López reaches across and finger taps the underlined word.
'So, there was a plot?'
My distorted face, doubled, is too much.
'Sorry, Detective, can you take off your shades?'
'What'd you say?'
'I'm asking if you will take off your shades, the refection is a little...'
'And I'm *telling* you, we're the ones doing the asking. Reflections are the least of your worries right now, you hear me?'
The fingers of Frazier's mutated hand drum the table. He gives it a moment before speaking.
'Tell us about Frankie, Mr Ryder.'

Main Street USA. Painted timber facades and ornate verandas. We enter Ma's Bakery through swinging louvre half-panels.

White light bounces off egg-yolk walls to haze a soft yellow. Sticky buns smile from a plate glass display, sweeten the sour aroma of ground coffee. I slouch onto a stool stranded between cabinets of varnished pine stuffed with tiny brown sacks of coffee beans. A pasty toddler heckles from a stroller, jelly-smeared face scrunching as he jerks against safety harness and points towards me.

'Ada'tu tareeqi!'

I recognise the words as Arabic but can't grasp their meaning from the basic phrases gleaned from Frankie.

'Ada'tu tareeqi! Hal beemkanek mosa'adati?'

Frankie places a cappuccino under my nose, licks a chocolate speckled froth moustache as he slices a crème doughnut in two.

'Dig in, sugar will do you good.'

The coffee is liquid heaven. I savour the first scalding sip on my tongue before letting it trickle down my throat like lava.

'Ada'tu tareeqi! Hal beemkanek mosa'adati?'

'Hey, Frankie, you hear that kid?'

'He's speaking Arabic.'

'You hear that too?'

'Of course.'

'What the hell do you mean, of course? What's he shouting?'

'I'm lost, can you help me?'

'I'm lost?'

'Mr Ryder!'

'I'm lost.'

'Mr Ryder!'

Frazier glares, points his pen.

'Who's Frankie?'

'Frankie's a hero.'

'A hero?'

'Purple hearts, all that shit.'

'Frankie's in the military?'

'Yeah, he's in the military, just back from Helmand.'

'What's his last name?'

'You haven't IDed him?'

'For the final time, we'll ask the questions, Mr Ryder.'

'This hombre's one dumb fuck.'

'I thought you'd have his dog tags.'

'What's his family name?'

'Eagle.'

López stands. My melted faces zoom in.

'You fucking with us?'

'Don't fuck with us, Mr Ryder.'

'That's his name. Apache blood.'

She straightens, takes off shades, hooks them into shirt pocket. Frazier scrawls 'Apache' beneath Frankie's name. He tears the page from his notebook, hands it to López. She strides to the door, yanks it open, barks into the corridor.

'Hey, Murphy.'

A man's voice. López hands over the page, shuts the door. She slouches around the desk to stand behind me. Frazier resumes.

'You and Frankie friends for long?'

'Since we were kids. Can I get some juice?'

'You said there was a plot.'

'I really need some juice.'

'López, will you get Mr Ryder a glass of water?'

'Not water. Juice.'

López grabs my shoulder.

'Listen, dickhead. You're in no position to be fussy. You'll take what we goddamn give you.'

'Medicinal purposes. Blood sugar.'

I slump onto the desk. Formica ice against cheek. Frazier's watch reads five after ten. It's water-resistant to two hundred meters. López yanks me upright. Stars swirl through viscous air.

'I'm not going to tell you again...'

'I need juice.'

'Lord have mercy. López. Get Mr Ryder some juice.'

López marches from the room.

'Your juice is on the way, Mr Ryder.'

Frazier's eyes squint like I've shifted out of focus. Sweat rivulets. Stomach cramps. Head spins. Forehead sinks back onto cool Formica.

We're surrounded by dwarves. I pivot, fists poised, adrenaline surging, scan for Grumpy. He'll throw the first punch. I'm grabbed from behind.

'What are you doing?'

'Doing? Protecting myself. Little bastards are everywhere.'

'You gotta stop hassling kids.'

'Kids? Not kids. Dwarves.'

Coloured letters tumble from Frankie's lips.

'T-h-e-y-a-r-e j-u-s-t c-h-i-l-d-r-e-n.'

I squint surroundings into focus. Balls, beach balls, shelves stuffed with beach balls, each beach ball depicting the bulging face of a dwarf.

'It's a store, Frankie. It's a souvenir store.'

Frankie strides down an aisle towards what looks like a gleaming arc of swords. I mooch after him, knees at right angles to my general direction. Stocked shelves whizz by on either side, generating a strong headwind. I arrive exhausted to Frankie's side. They're swords alright, everything from claymore to samurai to Gurkha to corsair in a lavish semi-circular display. I go to place a hand on Frankie's shoulder. I'm face down on a wiry carpet. Roll over, scramble to my feet, stagger backwards, sideways, impossible to move forward. I drop to my knees, crawl to where Frankie stands engrossed in the display, oblivious to my struggle. A medieval knight in full armour stands to one side. My bewildered face refracts in the polished suit as I rise. Laboured breath clouds its breastplate. I catch my wind, turn to Frankie.

'Swords?'

'Swords.'

'Swords?'

He tears his gaze from the wall.

'I know they're swords.'

'Sorry.'

Frankie selects a succession of weapons, caresses ornate hilts, fingers rigid blades. I sense dwarves advancing through aisles, concealed behind stacked tack, prepping an ambush. Frankie swings a claymore two-handed, twisting and swirling as he chops and thrusts.

'This is the one.'

He checks his watch.

'Almost time.'

Frankie replaces the sword, marches towards the checkout. I swing down an adjacent aisle. One flank covered. Almost time? Time for what? Is there a plan? I rotate left and right so as not to be blindsided. A ginger-haired boy stares as I pass. Boy? I'm about to tear the mask from his dwarf face when Frankie materialises.

'I need your credit card.'

'Credit card?'

'You got it?'

'Don't know.'

'Check your wallet.'

'For what?'

Frankie dips into my pocket. I follow him to the counter, backwards, to keep an eye on Ginger. Little fuck will slice us with an axe if given an opportunity. A mouse-eared assistant hands Frankie a long parcel.

'Thank you, Mr Ryder. We hope you enjoyed your visit to Disney World. You drive safely now, ya hear'

We exit onto Main Street USA. It has quietened considerably.

'We going home?'

'Not yet.'

'Where's everybody?'

'The Palace.'

'The Palace?'

'For the countdown.'

'Countdown?'

Frankie bolts up the street. I jog to keep up, pursue him into a cheering cluster of waving miniflags. We barge through stubborn shoulders. An acne-speckled chub stabs me with the sharp end of his candy floss stick. I grab it, elbow his chin. He slumps onto me for a moment before sliding to his knees. A bald monstrosity of a man with a hippo's foreleg for a neck grabs my shoulder with a 'Hey, asshole.' I thrust the timber spike backward into his balls. He squawks like a kicked turkey, releases his grip as girandolas blast overhead to spew red, blue and white sparkles over the assembled. We burst through at the foot of the palace steps, jostle to hold position.

'Your juice, Mr Ryder. Mr Ryder?'

A carton of orange juice, three plastic cups, pitcher of ice. I fill a cup, down it in two gulps. Nothing has ever tasted this good. I drop ice cubes into the cup and refill.

'I hope Florida's Natural is okay, your highness. I didn't have time to squeeze fresh oranges.'

López flops down like a woman who's just run a four-minute mile. Frazier pours half a glass for himself, eases a single ice cube into the juice before resuming.

'You married, Mr Ryder?'

'No.'

'In a relationship?'

'Not right now, no.'

'The address on Mai Tai Drive, family home?'

'Yes.'

'Who else lives there?'

'I live alone.'

López straightens, places palms on desk.

'You just told us it's a family home.

'It is, was. My mom passed away this year, August the fourteenth.'

'Your father?'

'I never met my father.'

'Only child?'

'I have a half-sister. She lives in Jupiter.'

López leans back, folds arms. Frazier downs his juice, gestures with the plastic cup.

'You in gainful employment, Mr Ryder?'

'Not at the moment.'

'You majored in philosophy at Florida State.'

'That might be the reason.'

'Reason for what?'

'Not being in gainful employment.'

López rests head in hands before eyeing me once more.

'You said Frankie lost the plot. What plot was that, exactly?'

'It's an expression.'

'There was no plot?'

'We were just out for New Year's Eve.'

'Why the Magic Kingdom?'

'Frankie wanted to go there.'

'You didn't?'

'I suggested Universal.'

'Why?'

'For a change; better rides... Magic Kingdom is for kids.'

'You don't like kids, do you, Mr Ryder?'

'What makes you say that?'

'You assaulted a child last night, almost blinded him.'

'I thought he was Dopey.'

'So, you poked him in the eye?'

'It was an accident.'

'The kid has a scratched cornea.'

'Sorry to hear that. Like I said, it was an accident.'

'You said The Magic Kingdom was Frankie's idea.'

'He insisted on it.'

'Why?'

'To strike at the heart of the beast.'

'What does that mean?'

'Who knows? Frankie often speaks like that. He likes metaphorical language.'

'And you just went along with it?'

'I hadn't seen Frankie in four months. I didn't care where we went.'

Disney characters assemble along the platform, waving hands and wagging mid-riffs. The opening bars of 'Frosty the Snowman'. Frosty skips along the front of a cartoon menagerie as the track kicks in, high-fiving Mickey, Minnie, Pluto, Chip, Dale, Donald, Daisy and Goofy before swinging towards the crowd and prancing foot to foot with jazz hands.

I look up towards battlements. A honey-haired damsel in billowing cream gown waves from a moon window near the top of one tower. She's imprisoned. I feel her pain, her desperation, condemned to watch powerless over this kingdom of deplorables. I'll need a grapple hook and length of knotted rope to have any hope of rescuing her. Adventure Land is the most likely source of climbing gear.

We're into countdown. Wheels and crowns shoot, burst and cascade over the whooping congregation.

Happy New Year!

'Auld Lang Syne'. Mickey and Minnie swing hand in hand, nose to nose. Chip and Dale bounce about, paws in the air. Woody and Jessie skip along the top step. Donald waddles waving across the platform, farting senseless sentences from his orange bill, white-feathered backside exposed to all. A flash of polished steel. Donald's impaled on a claymore. His body scrunches as the sword sinks to the hilt, stretches upward when the steel pulls from his chest. Flatulent bill briefly silhouettes in the lilac glow of the palace. He tumbles forward down steps, bounces off belly to flip onto his back, spasmodic jerks of splayed legs his final dance. Mania surges through the throng. I'm down. Trampled as I squirm. Forehead thumps onto polished brick. Nose scrunches into the sticky mustard of a flattened hotdog.

'Was the LSD Frankie's idea?'

'What's that?'

'The LSD. Frankie's idea?

'No, sir.'

'Your idea?'

'It wasn't anybody's idea. Just happened.'

López fist slams the table. My insides twang like a mariachi band hyped on Adderall.

'You playing us for fools?'

'Don't play us for fools, Mr Ryder.'

Deep breaths. Settle jitters. Mouthful of juice. So cold, so beautifully cold.

'Mr Ryder?'

'There was no plan. It was New Year's Eve. We were hitting the Magic Kingdom. It was the obvious thing to do.'

'The obvious thing to do?'

'We'd done it before.'

'LSD?'

'All of it. Tripping at Disney World. It was our thing. When we were in high school, we'd go at the weekends. It was just a thing.'

'Where'd you get the LSD?'

'A guy.'

'A guy?'

'Downtown.'

'His name?'

'Never got his name.'

'Listen, you're in a world of shit, now isn't the time to hold out on us.'

'We never got his name.'

'What did he look like?'

'Average height, average build.'

'Stop fucking with me.'

'A man died, Mr Ryder.'

'You think I don't know that? I was there.'

'The sale of LSD is a crime. It led to a murder.'

'Donald Duck was killed by a US marine. A patriot.'

They eye one-another like I've divulged new information. These dicks are amateurs. López grabs her juice and walks away, looks towards the high window as she downs it. She returns, leans in from a standing position.

'Not Donald Duck, Mr Ryder. Pedro Barrera. Pedro Barrera was killed by an assailant high on LSD.'

'He also had a sword. You going to arrest the person who sold the sword?'

López sits, breathes deep and slow.

'Pedro Barrera was father to three young children. You know what it's like to grow up without a father, don't you, Mr Ryder?'

She leans back into her chair.

'You have military training, Mr Ryder?'

'What's that got to do with anything?'

'I asked you a question.'

'No.'

'Why's that?'

'I'm not in the military.'

'You wanted to be.'

'Not really.'

'No?'

'You've checked my records. I don't see the relevance.'

'You failed the medical.'

'I failed the medical.'

'What grounds?'

'You know.'

'Maybe I want you to tell me.'

'You like being told things you already know?'

'How about I tell you this? Any more smart-ass remarks, and I'll bounce you off these four walls.'

'Maybe you need a psychological evaluation.'

López stands, fists clenched. Frazier takes over.

'How did you feel?'

'When?'

'When you failed the evaluation.'

'Relieved.'

'Relieved?'

'I'm not a killer.'

'And Frankie?'

'What about him?'

'Is he a killer?'

'He won two purple hearts. He just butchered Donald Duck. What do you think?'

'What about when you were kids?'

'There was something about him.'

'Violent?'

'Didn't need to be, you just knew.'

'Knew what?'

'Not to fuck with him.'

'What was he like after?'

'His tours?'

'Yeah.'

'Different.'

'Different?'

'More philosophical, asking questions.'

'Did he ask you questions?'

'All the time.'

'About what?'

Rap on door. It eases open. Murphy beckons with arched mono-brow. López taps Frazier on the arm. He turns off the recorder and follows. Murmurs as I splurge on juice. Where the fuck is Frankie? What can they charge me with? Use of an illicit substance? Hardly a biggie. Aiding and abetting? Serious shit. These fucks will try to pin something heavy on me.

The baby nods to affirm Frankie's translation. Its mother reaches over to wipe jelly from its face with a floral napkin. Flab dangles from the back of her upper arm, swings to and fro as she works. Frankie's lemur eyes reflect my scepticism as he leans in.

'He's from the future.'

'The future?'

'Or the past. Doesn't matter.'

'There's a difference between future and past.'

'Neither exist, irrelevant which he comes from.'

'Neither exist?'

'They're only words, concepts.'

'If he's from the future, and the future doesn't exist, then he can't exist either.'

'Exactly.'

'We're sitting here listening to him, man; we're sitting here listening to him, here and now, in the present. The present exists.'

'The present connects two non-entities, therefore becomes a non-entity itself.'

'None of this is real?'

'Look out at the street.'

Donald Duck waddles past the open door, cackle of children milling around his white-feathered ass.

'What do you see?'

'Donald.'

'On his own?'

'With a mob.'

'Why would a mob follow Donald? He's unintelligent, temperamental, farts incessantly through that orange bill, struts about in public naked from the waist down; treats Daisy like shit.'

'They're kids.'

'Kids can be pretty discerning.'

'Donald's famous, he's on TV and shit.'

'You think this is really Main Street USA, that Ma's in the kitchen baking apple pie and Cinderella lives in the palace at the top of the street?'

'Of course not.'

'Why not?'

'It's an illusion, fantasy.'

'But when you're here a while, it becomes real.'

'I'm always aware of the illusion.'

'You just poked a kid in the eyeball.'

'I thought he was Dopey.'

'So, you poked him in the eye?'

'Ada'tu tareeqi! Hal beemkanek mosa'adati?'

Frankie rests his forearms on the table.

'What if I was to tell you it is. Main Street USA. Right here, right now. This is the reality.'

'You're tripping.'

'In here, things are as they should be. Mobs are exclusive to children, and adults are here to ensure they don't get out of hand. Outside of here. That's the illusion.

'Ada'tu tareeqi! Hal beemkanek mosa'adati?'

'Two individuals distort their consciousness. Both hear a toddler shouting Arabic. How is that possible?'

'Fuck knows.'

'It's a single consciousness, creating its own world.'

'A dream?'

'Not *a* dream, your dream.'

'You don't exist?'

'I exist in your consciousness. You're creating the world as you go, shooting your own movie.'

I stand. Swipe hands across in front of my chest.

'Cut. Cut the fucking thing. I'm sick of it.'

'I didn't say you were directing, only shooting.'

'Who's directing?'

'You do realise you're asking yourself that question?'

'Fuck you, Frankie. I direct myself. I've always directed myself.'

I dart over to the baby, hunker so we're face to face. Jelly clogs its left nostril. Steeples blaze deep in its pupils.

'Ada'tu tareeqi! Hal beemkanek mosa'adati?'

'You and me both, kid.'

'Ada'tu tareeqi! Hal beemkanek mosa'adati?'

'Can't even help myself.'

'Hey, what's the matter with you?'

Hip-slung breasts bounce me from the child. Mom towers over my prostrate figure. Her face has the look and texture of a worn baseball mitt cupped for a catch. She shapes to stomp my nuts into the varnished floorboards. Frankie steps over me.

'Sorry, Mam, he didn't mean anything. Has a brother that age.'

'What's wrong with that man?'

'Just a couple of beers too many, Mam. I'm taking him home.'

'Why does he look like that?'

Frankie places a hand on her shoulder and leans in close. They look down at me, flailing on my back like a flipped turtle.

'My friend has special needs, Mam.'

She sits. Timber shudders beneath. Frankie bends and scoops me off the floor.

'C'mon, buddy, time we got you home.'

Door slams. Frazier and López retake their seats. Frazier drops a sheaf of documents onto the desk. A chainsaw whines in the distance. López hits record.

'Exactly when did you take the LSD, Mr Ryder?'

'The line for Space Mountain.'

'Why there?'

'Fifty-minute wait. Figured we'd be coming up by the time we got on the ride. The mountain would do the rest'

'The rest?'

'Adrenaline would speed up the process, shoot us sky-high.'

'Did it work?'

'Hell yeah.'

'Then what?'

'We bounced like pinballs around Future Land.'

'You progressed to It's a Small World.'

'Progressed might be too strong a word.'

'Why there?'

'Just where we ended up.'

'No reason?'

'No.'

'Why did you enter?'

'Why not?'

'It's a goddam ride for toddlers, that's why not.'

López is close enough to kiss. She smells of chocolate milk.

'You a toddler, Mr Ryder?'

'No, Mam.'

'Forgive the sarcasm of my partner, My Ryder. Detective López is finding it difficult to ascertain motivation. It seems unusual for a grown man to enter It's a Small World.'

'Two grown men. We just went with it.'

'Frankie's idea?'

'No.'

'Just went with it. What does that mean?'

'Went with the trip. Just one of those things. We regretted it. That's one freaky ride.'

Frazier flips through the bundle, selects a page.

'You said Frankie purchased the sword.'

'In the souvenir store.'

'The sword was purchased with your credit card.'

'Frankie borrowed my card. Didn't realise what he was buying. I was in an aisle. It was in a box.'

'You just gave him your card?'

'He took it. Really, I'm not shitting you. Check the CCTV.'

Frazier sniggers. López waits for it to peter out.

'Exactly when did Frankie return home?'

'Morning of New Year's Eve.'

'Just turned up at your door?'

'He likes to surprise.'

'When had you last seen him?'

'August thirtieth. Night before he shipped out.'

'You do anything?'

'Went to the Magic Kingdom. Like I said, it's our thing.'

Frazier puts the page down, extracts a photo, places it face-up on the desk.

'Tell me what you see, Mr Ryder?'

The shot is quality. No cheap surveillance at Disney. I need to drop a few pounds.

‘I’m in line for Space Mountain.’

‘Anything strike you as unusual?’

‘No, just me in line.’

‘Just you in line?’

Silence as they stare. Frazier’s cell phone vibrates. He extracts it from his pocket, looks at the screen, places it on desk. It buzzes and spins like a concussed bee before falling silent. López jabs at the photo.

‘Well?’

‘I’m standing in line, what of it?’

‘Anything missing?’

‘Frankie. He’s out of shot.’

Frazier extracts a second photo. It’s one of those gimmicky tourist shots Disney peddle after rides. It’s a Small World. I’m in the barge. A saucer-eyed Gollum.

‘This isn’t right.’

‘Why’s that, Mr Ryder?’

‘You’ve doctored the image.’

‘What’s wrong with the image?’

‘Frankie’s been erased.’

López stands and walks away from the desk, tucks shirt in. Badge catches slant of sun as she leans against the wall. Noose shadows over her head. Frazier leans in, clear snot snail slime through moustache. His left eyelid flickers.

‘I’ve told you all I know. You going to charge me? ’Cause if not...’

López strides to the desk.

‘Shut the fuck up.’

‘I want a lawyer.’

Frazier slides a photostat across the desk. It’s a page from the *Orlando Sentinel*. There’s a picture of Frankie. He’s in uniform.

'What's the publication date of this newspaper, Mr Ryder?'

'I can't read it.'

López sighs.

'Now he can't read.'

'The acid. Letters running around like ants.'

López scrapes chair to desk and sits.'

'How about I read it for you? Tuesday, December thirty-first, 2019. Yesterday.'

'Why's Frankie in it?'

López bristles. Frazier rests a hand on her wrist. He places a finger on the caption beneath the photo. I squint, attempt to gather the letters into some semblance of order. Nausea returns. I throw back a mouthful of juice, close one eye. López turns the photostat, reads the caption.

'Decorated war hero, Gunnery Sergeant Frank Eagle, US Marine Corp, killed while on active service in Afghanistan.'

I spew juice onto the page. López springs from her chair. Frazier remains still, ignores the splatter. I push back from the desk. A drawer opens. Frazier flings paper napkins onto the floor, mops the desk. Acidic stench spears nostrils. I'm yanked upright, Frazier blurred through tears, septic purr of López by my ear.

'Mr Ryder. Frank Eagle died of a single gunshot wound in Helmand province on the morning of December thirtieth.'

'No. Not possible.'

'The news aired on WFTV the morning of December thirty-first.'

'You're full of shit.'

Frazier slides another photo across the table.

'Do you recognise this individual?'

López pushes my head closer. Tears blur vision. I blink, watch them trickle along my nose to drip onto the bare-chested figure in the photo.

'It's me.'

'Where are you?'

'On the steps of the palace.'

López jabs the image.

'And what's that in your hand?'

'A sword.'

'A bloody sword, Mr Ryder. And who is that lying at your feet?'

López rests a hand on my right forearm.

'Jack Ryder, I am arresting you for the murder of Pedro Barrera. You have the right to remain silent. If you give up your right to remain silent, anything you say can and will be used against you in a court of law. You have the right to have an attorney present. If you cannot afford an attorney, one will be appointed to represent you. Do you understand? Mr Ryder, have you anything to say?'

Poised pen snug against Frazier's half thumb. I point to the damsel silhouette high behind my sword-wielding doppelganger.

'The girl.'

'The girl?'

'In the castle. The girl in the castle. I never got to rescue her. I never got to rescue anybody.'

Sacred Streams of Balaji Dham

The Sadhu leans across JD to spit vile, red phlegm over my lap and through the open window, viscous string trailing after the glob like a comet's tail. JD's sunburnt beak remains buried in his *Lonely Planet* guide, sluicing a steady trickle of begrimed sweat onto its pages. I nudge his shoulder, unload into his peeled ear.

'I'll hit that lad a dig if he doesn't stop.'

'Will you stop letting it rise you. Just ignore him.'

JD's index finger dawdles along cluttered lines of text, his chilled demeanour at odds with the oppressive heat.

'Eleven hours he's been at it.'

'You can't hit a Sadhu. He's sacred.'

'Everything's sacred to someone in this place.'

JD pauses his finger, regards me for a moment, adopts his schoolmaster tone.

'The Sadhu is sacred to everyone.'

He returns to his reading. Finger dawdles along once more. Perhaps I should hit JD a dig. JD's not sacred to anyone.

Now the collision drama is passed, our fellow passengers turn towards us and resume their collective gawk. Faces shimmer through gritted, syrupy air as deranged debate clatters around the decrepit bus, a chorus cackling into and over one another as they speculate upon the prospects of the two pasty lumps broiling in the corner. They appear to be placing bets on the exact moment I'll break. A turnip-shaped man sporting a glossy yellow tunic and broken teeth is the designated bookmaker. He guffaws and points towards me, as one would at a caged chimpanzee shaping to fling its faeces at a bunch of schoolchildren.

'Don't give them the satisfaction.'

JD raises an eyebrow towards me.

'Don't give who the satisfaction?'

'They're still staring.'

He glances up, buries beak in the text once more.

'It's just their way.'

Shouts from the bustling street as tumbled tuk-tuk is hoisted upright. Its dazed jockey accepts tiger balm from a woman in a maroon sari. Three men jabber at our driver as they gesticulate towards a vehicle with so many dents, it would be impossible to identify any recent additions.

A naked wisp of a boy silhouettes in the doorway of a ramshackle galvanised shack. He spots my white face, squints through the choking ochre haze churned up by a cacophony of garish trucks blaring through the village. Another hack and spit from the Sadhu, another glob whizzes past my nose. A one-eared hound, scavenging through rotted peels, yelps when the crimson spittle splats its forehead. It darts past the boy into the shack. A scrawny black heifer bolts out through the doorway, skitters to a halt upon catching sight of our bus, raises its tail, and spews a colossal amount of teal-green shit onto the head of the boy. The boy barely flinches, maintains eye contact as glutinous excrement steams down over him like molten lava, its pungent perfume routing the stench of diesel fumes and baked garbage. He raises a hand and flicks a glob from above his left eyebrow, the smooth casual action of one resigned to being stranded in an incessant deluge of steaming shit.

The bus lurches forward. Pots, pans, and squawking poultry cascade from above. JD screams as he parries the whirring claws of a riled rooster, shreds of his precious guidebook confetti in its wake. He grips my arm.

'You're right. This place is insane. We'll never survive two months.'

The bus shifts gear. Its exhaust blasts a noxious plume of dust towards the boy. He splutters as it settles like flung paprika on the glistening streams oozing down face and torso. I turn to JD.

'We'll be alright.'

The Sadhu hacks and spits.

'We'll be alright.'

Nothing to Be Done

Eight months. Eight months of culls, nets, patrols, shootings. Still, the seals return, sleek scavengers rising to the jackhammer pulse of a city's ruptured slumber, eyes sparking emerald through luminescent foam which swirls like wild sleet in sweep of halogen beam. How often did we sit and watch? Watch the chopper swoop down over the estuary? Watch the lifeboat plunge through agitated waves? Watch muzzle flash herald each flat futile crack.

Here we go, you said, the night of our exam results, another poetic ending. That one got me. Long time since you'd scored a rise, but that one got me. What's poetic about it? That condescending smirk as you took a final hit and flicked roach into water. Think of what they become – seal shit in the sea. Don't tell me that's not poetic. I wanted to throw you in after the roach, say something like, 'How's that for poetic, asshole.' I was too mangled to get it together but ran the scene in my mind. The sudden heave off the bench, kick up the arse for good measure, your arc through the air, the glorious splash, your outrage breaking the surface, freezing stab gasps as you flounder towards the pier. How's that for poetic?

Stood on O'Brien's Bridge last night, gazed upon the indifferent beast, ripples and eddies ruffling its pelt as it roared to the bay. Its roar sounds like applause at full flow. I never noticed before. Tumultuous applause, applause demanding an encore, applause which buoyed me down to the Sparch. Saw us sharing a bottle of Buckie, legs dangling over the bank, grey heron a sullen sentry in the shallows. Continued out by the Claddagh, round the back of the Swamp, along the shore, building fires there on summer nights, sipping the whiskey wisdom of wandering soothsayers drawn to our beacon. Walked the prom, out as far as the cliffs, us skittering in the dip on the edge, beneath the wind, above the jewelled bay, waves crashing as gulls swoop and squawk, too stoned to make our way back, too stoned to care.

Waiting for Godot at The Black Box: four weeks ago tomorrow. Marie surprised me with those tickets; didn't expect a graduation gift. Reward for her two favourite men, she said. I still don't get it, by the way. Don't get why it was sold out, why Beckett was a genius, why you were so taken by it. Wide-eyed, silent, first to stand and applaud, I thought you'd been hypnotised. Not a word until The Blue Note, halfway through our pints. Wasn't that just amazing? Did you ever see a better play? I wasn't having that. Nothing happened. That damn smirk as you leaned in. Nothing ever happens, Sean.

Saw Marie twice today, and yesterday, and the day before. Through the window, that is, on her way to work, on her way home. She phoned a couple of times. Can't face speaking with her yet, just sit here at the window and wait for her to pass, missing her every minute, wanting to be with her, to share with her, something, I don't know. I sound like your mother's stalker. I'll give her your note soon. When did you leave that, by the way? Before we headed out to wait for that bollocks, Godot?

Speaking of mothers, you dragged mine back, if nothing else, brief dip into her secret life. She's only gone and got herself a boob job. The old fella broke out at the sight of them. Snatcher Molloy is telling everyone Bridie's knockers knocked Puke McGowan off the wagon. I've hardly seen him since, the old fella, that is. Propping up the bar in Murphy's, no doubt. It's peaceful in the house without him blustering about the place, muttering and moaning.

It's fucking biblical outside. Massive contrary clouds swept in this afternoon to put the day out of its misery, rain like flung gravel against the glass since. My therapist suggested talking to you, in case you're wondering. I have a therapist now. How grown up is that? I know what you'd say. You'd say, how fucked up is that? And rant about pseudoscience and first world problems. The sessions were a parting gift from my mother. Nothing says I care like paying a stranger to listen to me. She's nice in fairness, the therapist, I mean. Talking passes time if nothing else. Time feels skewed, turned in on itself, hostile, I don't know. If you were here, we'd skin up and shite-talk concepts of time into the early hours. If you were here, it'd be a third friend in the room, indulging our half-arsed notions.

I will give Marie your note. It's just... Mad to think I'm avoiding Marie, of all people. First thing she said to me: Where were you, Sean? She didn't mean anything by it, I know that, unusual for one of us to be without the other. She hugged me then, hugged me for a long time, face damp on my neck, vanilla musk rising with the warmth of her. Sorry, slipped into stalker mode again. I will make sure your mother gets the note.

Rain's stopped. Water surges through drains and gullies, flushing the weary veins of this disorientated city, this sinking city, this city waiting to drown. The indifferent beast will roar tonight. Tumultuous applause will resound through drenched mournful streets. Sleek scavengers will rise to jackhammer pulse. Eyes will spark emerald in sweep of halogen beam. Sleet spray will swirl luminescent into black. A brief raucous denouement to a play in which nothing happens. I might wander down shortly.

Capital Vices

Mark downs the remainder of his third Guinness. He places his empty pint glass to one side of its coaster and circles a crossword clue a third time. His glass is plucked from the table.

'Another pint?'

Mark remains engrossed in his crossword for a moment before glancing up at the bartender.

'Please.'

Mark returns to the crossword. The bartender's red Converse trainers remain stationary, vivid against the drab carpet.

'What are you stuck on, then?'

'Not stuck, just can't recall the answer.'

'If the clue is "definition of stuck," that's your answer right there.'

Mark puts down his pen, sits back, looks into moist mismatched eyes. Sculpted eyebrows are set at indifferent, the right one pierced with a silver hoop that reflects the stacked glasses tucked into her right shoulder.

'Deadly sins. Two words, seven letters and five, second letter is A.'

'Seven and five?'

'Yes. Second letter is A.'

'Capital vices.'

'Capital vices?'

'Pride, greed, lust, envy, gluttony, wrath and sloth. The seven deadly sins, also known as capital vices.'

She leans into Mark and whispers.

'The sins which lead to ruination.'

She straightens and strides towards the bar, Mark's gaze following her. He turns back to his crossword, catches a flash of lilac through the half-light of the arched entrance to the bar. Tilt of her chin. The swish and bluster of her gait. Mark is fifteen, back at St Andrew's, enduring detention by rain-streaked windows. Penelope squeezing in beside him on a slipstream of attitude, her ragged lilac scarf a streak of cheer through the drab afternoon.

'Are you going to offer me a seat?'

'Penelope. Sorry, off in my own world.'

'Simone, Mark. My name is Simone.'

'What? Of course, Simone. What did I say?'

'You said Penelope. Thought the least I could expect is that you'd know my name after eight months.'

'Sorry, babe, don't know what I was thinking.'

'Who's Penelope?'

'What?'

'Penelope. Who is Penelope?'

'I don't know any Penelope. Must have heard the name somewhere.'

'Why are you blushing?'

'I'm not blushing.'

'Yes, you are. Bright red.'

'I am now. Because you said I was blushing.'

Mark stands, reaches into his pocket.

'Want a drink?'

Simone stares for a moment, milking the last of the interrogation. She sheds a damp cream Macintosh and throws it over the back of a chair. Scarf a sleek guppy's tail over right shoulder, lips and eyelids tinted to match, black pencil lines and long lashes stark against alabaster skin stretched taut across sharp cheekbones by her grimace.

'Yeah, go on, I need one after the day I've had.'

'Gin and tonic?'

'Have you ever known me to drink anything else?'

'Just being polite.'

'I'm just thankful you remembered.'

Amber spotlight pierces the soft cotton of Simone's blouse. A man ogles from a high-stool perch, grey suit skewed on simian frame, tight across shoulders with cuffs a third of the way up long sinewy forearms. He turns a dented face to Mark as the bartender places a Guinness on the counter beside a gin and tonic.

'You alright, mate?'

'Alright. You?'

'Couldn't be better, mate.'

He nods towards Simone.

'Fit bird your missus.'

'Yes, she's very attractive.'

'Married?'

'Not yet, no.'

'You're engaged then?'

'I don't know if...'

''Cause I don't see no stone.'

'No, well...'

'Not too happy with you, mate.'

'Actually, we're very happy, couldn't be happier if you must know.'

'Don't mean no offence, mate, just making conversation.'

Mark picks up the drinks and turns from the bar.

'Well, if you'll excuse me.'

Mark places the drinks in front of Simone. He drags his chair around and sits to obstruct the view.

'Tough day?'

'Don't talk to me.'

'Adam?'

'The man hasn't a clue. What is it about managers?'

It's not just the lilac scarf. Those olive-green eyes, and her face. Is it the make-up? It's more than that: the shape, the pert nose, in a certain light she could pass. How had he not noticed?

'Are you even listening to me?'

'Course I'm listening.'

'You're off in your own world.'

'Just thinking how you're wasting your talent with that crew. Adam's never going to take you seriously.'

'I know. Can you believe he said that?'

'The man hasn't a clue.'

'It's insulting, that's what it is, being objectified in that way.'

A waifish flame-haired woman in egg-yolk dungarees wrestles a house burger in an alcove behind Simone. She catches Mark's eye with mouth at reptilian stretch. Sauce-soaked burger tongue pokes through bread lips as she bites, spurting mayo over her fries.

'Where did you go to school?'

'As in secondary school?'

'Yes.'

'Why do you want to know?'

'Just curious.'

'Ealing Comprehensive.'

'All girls?'

'Mixed.'

'Uniform?'

'Yes.'

'What was it like?'

'I don't know. Like any other school, I suppose.'

'The uniform. What was the uniform like?

'Navy skirt – pleated – white blouse, red tie, blazer. Why?'

'No reason.'

'There's always a reason.'

'Just thinking maybe we could spice up our love life a little.'

'I wasn't aware it needed spicing up.'

'It doesn't. You know what I mean. Try something different.'

'I told you before, I'm not doing that.'

'Not that. I was thinking more of, you know, a little role play.'

'Role play?'

'With your uniform.'

'What are you, a paedophile?

'Of course not. Schoolgirls can be eighteen, you know.

'Schoolgirls can be eighteen, Mark, but I'm thirty-one, in case you haven't noticed. And you're thirty-four.'

'It's only a bit of fun.'

'It's bloody perverse, that's what it is.'

'You'd still pass for eighteen.'

Simone swells slightly and flicks hair from her forehead. She looks over her glass at Mark.

'That's not the point. It would be weird.'

'What's weird? We're consenting adults.'

'Let's just drop it, okay.'

'Okay.'

'I need another drink. You want a pint?'

'Please.'

Simone scrolls as she waits at the counter. The suited man leans towards her and speaks. She turns, finger poised on screen. He stands to shake her hand, forcing her to disregard the phone, then sits back down and passes a comment. She giggles, leans in with a retort as the drinks arrive. His pyroclastic guffaw cuts through the bustle like the deep, urgent woofs of a startled Labrador. The man retrieves his wallet from the bar, extracts a card and hands it to her. She places it on her phone, puts both into her handbag, adds tonic to her gin and grabs both glasses, flashing a smile as she turns from the bar. It still plays on her lips as she places drinks on coasters and sits.

'What did he say?'

'Who?'

'The gorilla at the bar.'

'Stewart. He's nice.'

'Stewart?'

'He's a fashion consultant.'

'Fashion consultant?'

'You just going to repeat everything I say?'

'No, it's just that...'

'What?'

'He looks more defendant than consultant.'

'He thinks I look younger too.'

'Course he does.'

She leans across the table, kisses him on the lips, lingers eye to eye with hand cupped around his neck.

'Is my little baby jealous of the strange man at the bar?'

'Why would I be jealous?'

Moist juniper lips, waft of dried raindrops, black strands clinging to the white of her neck. Mark draws her to him, teasing and probing until she commits to the kiss. Three striped shirts with beer bellies enter on a cool tobacco breeze.

'Oy, get a room, why don't ya?'

The men snigger as they pass. Simone picks up her drink and swirls the ice with her finger.

'You really think I'd pass for eighteen?'

'Told you I did.'

'So, you agree with Stewart?'

A smirk creases her left cheek. Mark wipes his lips with the back of his hand and places the pint to one side of its coaster.

'On this single occasion, I agree with Stewart, or to be precise, Stewart agrees with me.'

'Stewart agrees with you?'

'Let's just say, to avoid any argument, that on the subject of your youthful looks and all-round hotness, Stewart and I are in complete agreement.'

She leans to him, nestling into his shoulder.

'You're a clown, Mark Jones, you know that?'

'A really sexy clown?'

'Just a clown.'

She kisses him.

'Okay, I'll do it.'

'You'll do it?'

'The schoolgirl thing, I'll do it. It might be fun.'

‘Really? Tonight?’

‘I don’t have my uniform at the flat. I’m home Friday, how about the weekend?’

He kisses her earlobe, feels her leg quiver beneath his hand as he whispers.

‘Penelope.’

Mark attempts to mop the blinding sting with his shirt sleeve. The bartender appears and hands him a dry cloth. She moves Mark’s pint and paper to an adjacent table, picks up the empty lilac-smudged Slim Jim, whips out a second cloth, wipes in a furious counter-clockwise motion, flicking nuggets of ice onto the carpet. She returns Mark’s pint, placing it on a fresh coaster, and picks up the paper, perusing the crossword as Mark dabs around his neck and inside the front of his soaked shirt.

‘Portend.’

‘Sorry?’

‘Seventeen across. A sign or warning that something momentous or calamitous is likely to happen. Portend.’

She drops the paper onto Mark’s table.

‘Finished with the rag?’

A futile rub to his crotch and Mark hands the cloth over.

‘I’m Mark, by the way.’

‘Clotho.’

‘Clotho?’

‘Greek. My Mother’s from Athens’

Clotho tucks the rag into the belt of her apron and walks back towards the bar, gathering glasses as she goes. Mark looks after her, scans the room. The three striped shirts laugh and point, hunched into one another, midriffs quivering. The flame-haired woman in egg-yolk dungarees leans back into her alcove, pouring salt onto a ketchup splotch on her chest. Other customers feign interest in conversations or newspapers.

Mark returns to his crossword, fills in portend. Almost complete. One final clue remains unanswered. Fifteen down. Six letters. The three fates of Greek mythology – Lachesis, Atropos and... The C of Capital is the first letter, the O of Portend the third. He looks to where Clotho clinks glasses into a wash basket. A barely touched pint of lager glows from where Stewart had been. Clotho grabs it, empties the glass into the sink before adding it to the other empties and heaving the basket into the washer. She whips out her rag and wipes down the counter.

The Rise and Demise of Captain Club Milk

July '82. Six of us perched slurping from goons on the Happy Wall in Salthill. Zeno commented on the scrawny middle-aged man sneaking glances our way, each time lifting his lapel to mutter into a device of some kind. The man was nestled into a tangle of overhanging ivy at the entrance to Flea Lane. Navy anorak, navy slacks, blue shirt and black polished brogues, conspicuous attire on a rare sweltering Sunday.

Being under surveillance stoked adolescent aspirations. We were *Los Diablos*, scourge of Hill Street. Both Dobs and Slow-Mo fancied the role of Jesús Martinez, were wrestling the issue on the grass when Jasper strutted down Flea Lane, paused to peek inside the man's anorak, crossed to inform us the concealed device was in fact a Club Milk. A match inserted into the yellow outer wrapper of the chocolate-coated biscuit served as antenna, and a short length of copper wire curled from the base functioned as a mouthpiece.

From then on, whenever we jostled to the park or along the prom to go bushing, whenever we blustered into Galway to impose our mischief upon the town, Captain Club Milk would follow. No matter what day, no matter what night, no matter what time, his stooped decrepit figure would materialise in our wake to ghost along hedges and parked cars, skulk in doorways, stretch out on the rooftops of bus shelters, diligently relaying the group's movements via his makeshift walkie-talkie.

We floundered into late teens. Motorbiking replaced walking, and Captain Club Milk was unable to maintain his high level of surveillance. We'd occasionally spot him outside clubs at closing, squawking into his chocolate-coated biscuit as we wreaked havoc. In October '92, late one rowdy Saturday night, shades arrived in numbers, came at us with batons beneath a Hunter's Moon. Hyped on Scrumpy Jack and Billy Whizz, we battered them back to their squad cars. Captain Club Milk emerged from shadows to aid his beleaguered colleagues, sprinted full-tilt into the whirring night-stick of a bloodied sergeant. His prone figure almost flushed away on the torrent which gushed from his forehead.

Torch-beams flit frantic through the small church graveyard like roused ghouls as we huddled behind headstones and lay upon the unkempt graves of long-forgotten priests. An ambulance wailed its banshee wail from the street. A chopper thundered its way to Beaumont Hospital, its whirring throb fading as we crept through undergrowth past black polished brogues, their crackling walkie-talkies unable to relay the group's position back to headquarters.

Next morning, Zeno phoned to inquire. Critical care had no record of any Captain Club Milk.

Shadows

Barks from a side-shed as Tommy ambles through Moran's gate swinging a length of ash. Mick stops his chopping of logs, discards hatchet.

'The bould Tom Flah, just in time.'

'Time for what?'

'To get rid of the pups, auld fella's goin' mad.'

'Who'll take them?'

Mick picks up a hurl, tosses a stone into the air, strike a dry resonant crack, stone arcs over telephone cable into the thistle-plagued field across the road.

'Who in the name of Jesus wants those mongrels?

'Snipe again?'

'That dog is fuckin' deadly. A Jack Russell, how is it even possible?'

'Have to admire him, in fairness.'

Mick belts another stone into the field, drops hurl and walks back to the porch. Silver studs sparkle on the shoulders of his sleeveless denim jacket. He plucks a cloth potato sack from a window ledge. Tommy follows him into the side shed. Sheba woofs a welcome, plops paws onto the Phil Lynott silhouette spread-legged across Mick's deep chest. There's no mistaking the genetic history of the yapping litter. Every pup has the black hair and brown eyebrows of its father.

'Take a fair salesman to sell them as Golden Labradors.'

'Don't talk to me, and she locked in the shed. Thought I was seein' things when I opened the door to Snipe lookin' up at me, proud as a turkey cock.'

'Wonder ya didn't give it to him?'

''Twas the shock saved him.'

Mick opens the sack and feeds six whimpering pups to the darkness one by one. He grabs a length of baling twine off the boiler, pats a bewildered Sheba on the head, closes door and turns to Tommy.

'What happened the eye?'

'Walked into the door of the press, you know the high one in our kitchen, over the sink? Corner caught me.'

Mick roots through a small pile of rubble by the gable wall, selects half a concrete block, bangs it off the ground a few times and hands it to Tommy. He stoops and selects a slightly larger piece for himself.

'Looks a sore dose.'

'It's grand, had worse than this.'

Mick's rolling gait leads them through the lush boreen. Hawthorns bloom on either side, hunch over stone walls like farmers shooting the breeze, occasional blush tinting white blossoms. Grasshopper spit sprinkles brambles and ferns on either side. Sweet stench from the fresh dung splattered along the grass. They cut through a gap and follow a rabbit-run between clumps of heather. Mick's Doc Martens squelch on the soft ground. The sack yelps and gyrates in his right hand. They pause at a bog-hole. Tommy tests depth.

'Hardly enough.'

'Nah.'

'A child can drown in four inches of water.'

Mick looks to his friend.

'Next time we're drowning children, we'll use this one so.'

Their laughter unfurls along the springy heather, lightening the load in Mick's hand. He speaks back over his shoulder.

'I tell ya one thing, Sheila Joyce might avail of the service. Up the fuckin' stick again, can ya believe it?'

Mick pauses and looks back the way they came. A black smudge adorns his brow, turf dust from the floor of the shed.

'I tell ya, Flah, I wouldn't mind availing of her services.'

He looks skywards, loses himself in the vision. A thought brings him back.

'Who's the stallion this time? Hardly Podge Joyce again, is it?'

'Podge is in London for the past year. Putting down cable, he is.'

'Still pullin' his wire, so. I tell ya. When that bollocks can get a ride, there's hope for the rest of us.'

Tommy taps Mick on the shoulder with the ash.

'I know who the father is.'

'Who?'

'Can't believe we didn't cop it.'

Mick puts down the sack, drops block to ground, spreads turf dust across forehead with back of hand and waits, hands on hips, for the revelation. Tommy spreads arms wide.

'It's Snipe, who else? The little fucker's done it again.'

A blast of laughter shoots shockwaves back down along the boreen. Mick imitates Snipe going at it doggy style, little paws clutching onto Sheila as he thrusts.

'Oh, Snipe, you're so big, give it to me, please, more, more.'

He emits two yelps and a prolonged howl. They're on knees, clutching midriffs, struggling for breath. Two pups waddle, yapping from the sack. Mick makes a grab for the nearest one.

'Sheila's sprogs are getting away.'

Roll onto backs. Mick holds the escapee to his chest. It piddles down onto Phil Lynott. He flings it onto the heather. Tommy curls foetal, blue-green world swirls through salty tears as he struggles to control bladder. Each attempt at speech reignites the furnace until eventually, it burns itself out.

Mick reloads the sack, swings it over shoulder, picks up the block and tucks it under his free arm. They weave through clusters of flowering gorse, coconut scent sickly in the still air. Mick speaks without turning.

'You weren't in yesterday.'

'Nah.'

'How come?'

'Couldn't be arsed.'

'Missed fuck all, revision this and revision that, me sittin' there thinkin' I didn't see any of this shit first time round. All a load of bollocks if you ask me. Sure there's no work. What the fuck would ya want to be studying for?'

'English, Wednesday. Shouldn't be too bad.'

Mick swings around, eyebrows arch into black smudge.

'Not too bad? I tell ya one thing, Flah, I'll ram that exam so far up my hole, I'll be chewin' on it for a week, I mean for fuck's sake, sonnets? What good are sonnets to anyone? I wandered lonely as a cloud... Shakespeare my fuckin' arse.'

He resumes his trek across the bog. A robin joins them, hops from stalk to stalk alongside.

'That's Wordsworth.'

Mick leaves the bag down to readjust the block.

'What?'

'I wandered lonely as a cloud, that's Wordsworth.'

'Is that a fact? Wordsworth no less, and did he not write sonnets?'

'I don't know, Shakespeare wrote them anyway, 'cause that's what we're supposed to read.'

'Are we now, and have you been busy reading the bould Shakespeare in your spare time?'

Tommy laughs, drops his block, plucks a green reed from a clump at his feet, snaps the end off and places it into his mouth. He looks over the tip at Mick.

'I have in my arse. I just know The Daffodils, that's all.'

'The Daffodils?'

'Yeah, the Wordsworth poem, that's the only one I know.'

Mick spreads legs and leans back, glances at the whimpering bag at his left foot. A bee circles his head. He backhands it on the third lap to send it careening over the heather.

'What? Ya just love daffodils, is it?'

Tommy glances at the bag, takes reed from mouth, spits, wipes lips with the back of his hand, places reed in mouth, looks to where Galway Bay sparkles in the distance. He immerses himself in the view for a moment before turning back to Mick.

'The mother loved daffodils. She used to go on about that poem. I'd have to know it, wouldn't I?'

Tommy doesn't wait for an answer, leads over a pungent hoof-churned wet patch. They pause when back on solid ground. Black Jack rambles across a distant field, scarlet *geansaí Nollag* a beacon. Mick shakes his head.

'Gobshite loves that jumper.'

'Wouldn't do to walk near Lydon's bull wearing that.'

'That's not maybe. What time's the mass tomorrow?'

'Twelve.'

'Jesus, don't feel a year goin'.'

Tommy looks towards the sun, considers its trajectory. A heron rises twenty yards away, awkward and graceful, tucks head into shoulders with a sharp squawk as it traces a grey arc south. It alights near the tall pines behind Gannon's house.

'Down there his nest is.'

'Bet there's a decent hole up there.'

Mick points and walks towards where the bird rose. A brace of snipe break cover ten metres away, skim rushes, zigzag sharply, swoop at the far side of a slight mound. Tommy traces their brief flight with his stick.

'Have to get them before they turn, auld fella'd have them shot from the hip, Bang! Bang!'

'You any smokes?'

'Nipper.'

Tommy digs into pocket, produces half a mangled Major and a lighter. He sparks up the cigarette, inhales deeply, savours the head rush, exhales a rapid succession of rings through pursed lips, hands the fag to Mick and looks up at a jet powering towards the North Atlantic. Flotsam trails in its wake, slowly dissipating into nothingness.

'Another bunch gone, lucky fuckers.'

Mick blows smoke into swarming midges.

'Would ya go?'

'Be gone tomorrow if I could, out of this shithole.'

Mick sucks the dregs, flicks butt into mud, watches it smother, turns to his companion.

'Nice head on ya for New York. Your neck'd be fucked from lookin' up at the buildin's.'

Tommy lurches towards Mick, slips on soggy ground. Mick swivels, throws him over right hip onto grass. He places knee on Tommy's chest, slaps him across the face, mindful of the swollen eye.

'You'd want to be faster than that over there, boy, no second chances in New York City.'

Tommy grabs denim shoulders, swings Mick onto the bag of puppies.

Mick springs up like a goat, lands a foot each side of the squealing bundle.

Tommy rises, catches breath, retrieves block and length of ash. Sharp tobacco tang stalks them to where the heron rose. There's a pond, four-foot diameter, couple of foot deep in the middle, half-way up Tommy's staff. Green rushes encircle the brown water, and a smattering of bog-cotton sprinkles one side. Mick opens the sack and drops his block into the litter. Tommy flinches at the high-pitched yelps.

'Mind, you'll hurt the poor fuckers.'

'Think it matters at this stage?'

'No point making it worse.'

Tommy eases his block into the sack. Squashed little faces squint towards the light. Hopeful yaps intensify. Tommy turns to Mick pulling the baling twine from his back pocket.

'Is there no one who'll take them?'

'What's on ya, if ya can't stomach it, wait down there.'

Mick gestures towards the road. Tommy heaves the bundle to Mick's feet.

'Course I can stomach it, just a pity, that's all.'

Tommy steps to the bog-hole. A water boatman skims across his shadow. Two dragonflies chase one another, swoop to kiss water, emerald and scarlet candescent beneath blurred wings.

Mick's shadow merges from behind. The sack lands with a gulp. Insects surf splash-waves towards the peat perimeter. Tadpoles seek green slime at the edge. Glistening tails ruffle the surface.

The sack slowly sinks as soft water seeps through cloth to expel trapped air. Squeals become threads of tiny bubbles rising through murk. Sediment slowly settles. The sack belches one final time, loosens baling twine. A tiny black snout pokes through the slight opening, wriggles desperately into wet embrace. Mick shakes his head.

'Look at this bollocks?'

'You didn't tie it properly.'

'Course I fuckin' tied it properly.'

Mick calms when confronted by Tommy's smirk.

'There's always goin' to be a bit of give. It'll be grand.'

The pup's head breaks the surface, black eyes hysterical beneath brown eyebrows. He splutters in a circle like a dwarf sea-lion. Mick grabs the stick from Tommy.

'Fuck's sake.'

He places the point of the stick on the pup's crown and pushes him under. As they wait for the bubbles to cease, a sibling surfaces dead with lips curled back over virgin white teeth as if it grasped the comedy in its dying breath. Mick loses concentration, and his charge pops up once more to flounder towards the edge.

'Little fucker.'

Mick spears the pup into the side, drives him down into the murk, leaving weight on stick until he feels it pierce ribs. He looks wide-eyed at Tommy, yanks shaft from water with a loud 'Yeah!' Red tinges brown. A curlew sounds a keen from across the bog.

They shuffle around the pond until their shadows disappear, shutting the window. Tinted sky mirrors on water. Corpses float through wine-coloured clouds. Nymphs, water beetles and tadpoles dive into the murk. Water boatmen and pond skaters skim across the heavens. Tommy spots a frog camouflaged among reeds, throbbing throat compromising position. He says nothing.

They walk in silence back over the bog and down the boreen. The tommy-gun staccato of a roused tractor clatters in the distance. Mick glances at Tommy before he speaks.

'Hear your auld fella's back on the beer.'

'He is.'

'Since when?'

'Thursday night.'

Tommy looks across fields to where crows riot around a copse of spruce. He swings his ash, cleaves the prickly bulbous head off a thistle. It soars over a blackthorn. Mick's eyes follow the missile, return to his companion.

'You're quiet.'

'Thinkin', that's all.'

'They're better off, Tom. Nobody wanted the fuckers. If nobody wanted you...'

The boreen widens into the road. Tommy decapitates another thistle, swirls to Mick.

'Do ya know what the tragedy is?'

Tommy drops his ash and grabs Mick's shoulders.

'Do you know what the *real* fuckin' tragedy is?'

Mick shakes his head.

'How many males were in that litter?'

'Four.'

Tommy loosens his grip and stands back.

'Those four dogs will never get to enjoy the one God-given gift they possess.'

'How'd ya mean?'

'Don't ya get it, Mick? Those poor fuckers will never get to lick their own balls. The one thing that makes them better than us and we took it from them. Fuck your *Macbeth* and all that shite. That's a real tragedy.'

Tommy's guffaw is sudden and infectious. They bend double, teary-eyed, breathless. Mick places a hand on the back of Tommy's neck. He pulls him into a brief tight hug, pushes him away, punches hard into his right bicep.

Flashes

A flash: a thump to the back of his head. Ed sinks into a warm viscous flow as it slurps into a chasm. He teeters on the edge, slowly rolls over. Eyes jolt open. He's spewed from the chasm. Blinding glare. Tang of singed enamel. A voice from above.

ONE!

An operating theatre: masked surgeon in bright halo. Ed battles the anaesthetic, fears sinking, fears nothing. The Andaman Sea. Their honeymoon. Ascending towards surface glare. His measured breaths. Drone of engines through water.

TWO!

Flashes. Countless flashes. White sparks swirl into black. Inis Meáin: Summer '96. Stargazing by the cliffs. Gannets honk above. Waves thunder onto rocks below. Next stop, America. A fighter could do well there. If he had it in him. A figure stands over him.

THREE!

A referee. He's down. Head anchor-heavy on canvas which seems adrift on the swells west of Aran. The stinging jibes at the press conference. 'Do you think a man of your age can withstand the power of Tiger Lopez?' Flashes. Cameras shooting. Shooting. Recording his frailty.

FOUR!

Ed rolls onto his right shoulder, swivels onto one knee. The gym in Brockton: Goody beside him on the apron. 'Always take the count, son. If you're hurt, take the count.' A commentator spews into a microphone. 'He's down... Ed Joyce, the Man of Aran, is down in the first round here in Madison Square Garden. Tiger Lopez has one hand on the featherweight title.'

FIVE!

Ed runs into the dawn. Heaves icy air into deprived lungs. Vapour exhalations merge into the fingers of mist reaching up from the valley. He wills burning legs up steep slope. Goody's voice: 'Your pegs gotta be independent, son. When your brain is mush and your senses all fucked-up, your pegs need to stand alone.'

SIX!

A blood-speckled white shirt. Roar of the crowd. Stench of sweat and blood and leather. Punching the heavy bag as Goody preaches: 'You think they gonna hand you that title? No, siree, you gotta grab that motherfucka... No doubt.' The mantra beats through the gym in time with the combinations. 'No doubt. We ain't got no doubt.'

SEVEN!

An overhand right. Caught cold. Careless. Slow bringing back the jab. Ed looks to his corner. Flash of Goody's crooked smile. That was Tiger's best shot. They both know it. Tiger poised across the ring. Eyes ablaze with the desire to demolish a legend in front of the world. Ed shifts weight onto his left leg. Pushes off his knee.

EIGHT!

The arena erupts with his rise. The referee wipes gloves on shirt. 'You alright, Ed?' The arena swirls around three referees. 'Never been better.' A bellow from the corner: 'No doubt!' Ed inhales Goody's conviction with the bays of the mob. The referee shouts 'Box!' The arena soars toward crescendo. Tiger Lopez bolts into focus.

Gravediggers

We stand silent in the shed's shadow. Sipping dregs of tepid tea from cracked mugs, we shake the stiff from our legs, tobacco smoke sweet in the salt bluster. Whomper Daly's hip flask ghosts among us. Our tongues blaze brief and beautiful against the cold.

Platitudes pass through locals hunched beneath eaves.

'You never know.'

'No. You never know.'

The mantra of the blessed beats the creep of Colie's coffin along the flickering hallway. Fr. Keogh emerges, beseeches God to receive his loyal servant, flings holy droplets into dispassionate icy squall. Brass glows gold beneath porch light as brutal silhouette is coaxed through doorway. Maureen follows, face gaunt, bruises faint shadows through make-up. Set jaw of Lucy, father's portrait clutched to her chest, free hand upon the resolute shoulder of her mother.

A slip coming off the second step. Twist of Tom Fáda's spine. He catches the weight, rights the burden. Shone shoes crunch frosted pebbles in slow procession. Prayers blow asunder. An umbrella twists and flitters. Fr. Keogh's cassock rises, flaps feral above his head. Colie's coffin rolls smooth into gaping hearse. Wreaths ease in on either side. A bunch of white lilies placed on the box, fleet creamy clove whiff. Door shuts.

A late arrival. Fido McGowan with a skin full, jacket skew ways, glass eye luminescent through the gloom.

'Sorry for your troubles, Maureen. He'll be missed, I tell ya that for nothing. He'll be missed, will Colie.'

Oblivious to Maureen's glare, he slams a palm onto the roof of the hearse.

'Go n-éirí an bóthar leat, a chara.'

He rests his forehead on the rear window, weeps whiskey tears into the raindrop rivulets criss-crossing the glass. We stand silent in the shed's shadow. Silent: so as not to speak ill of the dead.

Whips, Spliffs and Larium at the Taj Mahal

Hawkers swoop as we exit the station. It's almost impossible to walk through as they pull at our sleeves and shout in our faces.

'I take you to Taj Mahal, good price.'

'Good price, my friend, I give good price.'

'You need guide, I show you Agra.'

'Red Fort, Taj Mahal, very cheap.'

'Taxi, Taxi, best price.'

I barge through to emerge onto a walkway which leads over a concrete bridge and onto a narrow rust-coloured dirt road. We pause to get our bearings and are engulfed again. A short, lithe man offers to sell me a black, leather whip for four hundred Rupees. Tassels dangle from the brass-studded handle of a soft coiled-leather whip of more use as a sex toy than for any Indiana Jones type shenanigans. The man beams up at me.

'For you, my friend, I make special price... Three-fifty Rupee.'

'Three-fifty, are you mad? I don't want.'

'You make me price, is very good, look.'

'I don't want a whip.'

'Okay, my friend, for you, three hundred Rupee.'

He shakes his head at being forced to sell at cost by my superior bartering technique.

'I give you fifty Rupee, no more.'

'Fifty Rupee, I cannot. Three hundred Rupee, best price. For you, my friend, special price.'

'Fifty Rupee, no more.'

I grab JD by the shoulder and jostle forward.

'Okay, my friend. For you, two hundred Rupee.'

'Fifty Rupee. No more.'

JD glares at me.

'Do we really need a whip?'

'Just getting rid of him. He won't go fifty.'

'Okay, fifty Rupee.'

He hands me the whip and awaits payment. Etiquette dictates I have to buy the damn thing. I give him a fifty and turn to deal with the manic throng. Standing before them with my man-friend and our sex-toy detracts from my credibility as a tough negotiator.

'You want taxi, my friend, to Taj Mahal?'

'No! Don't need taxi.'

'How you go?'

'We walk. We like to walk, no taxi.'

The men burst into laughter. The other tourists have been snatched up, which leaves us the sole chance of income until the next train arrives. Their laughter increases my determination to walk. I look around, expecting to see a white marble dome sparkling before me in the early morning sun. There's nothing but narrow grimy streets, a plethora of red brick, dirt road and galvanised roofs. The sun is building a head of steam. It won't be long before heat renders any notion of walking a folly. Drivers continue to pull at us and point towards their respective tuk-tuks as if they're numbered sex workers in a Thai go-go bar. I spot a scrawny man standing to the rear in silence and push through his colleagues to reach him.

'How much to Taj Mahal?'

'One hundred Rupee.'

'I give you twenty-five.'

'Twenty-five Rupee each.'

He points at each of us in turn by way of emphasis. Fifty Rupee seems to be the going rate, and nobody is willing to undercut this driver, at least not to an Irishman dumb enough to buy a useless leather whip within a minute of arrival into town. I nod agreement. We climb aboard the tuk-tuk and get on our way. A sinewy wisp of a man climbs aboard beside the driver and looks back at us. He has the face and demeanour of a weasel skulking around a henhouse in the dead of night.

'Hello, my friends. My name is Sanjog. I am your guide.'

'We no want guide.'

'I show you Taj Mahal, Red Fort, very cheap for you, my friends.'

'No thanks.'

'Where you go today?'

'Nowhere. We don't want guide.'

Sanjog's smile reveals uneven, crimson-blotted teeth. A Perspex amulet hanging from a leather necklace houses a tiny green Ganesh. He shakes his head, amused by our naivety. A dirty brown sow with sagging udders runs from the path of the tuk-tuk with four squealing piglets in pursuit. They jostle to snatch swinging teats as we putter deeper into winding streets lined by decrepit, white-washed homes caked in rust-coloured dirt churned up by passing traffic.

'Only one hundred Rupee. Special price for you.'

'No.'

'Where you from?'

'Doesn't matter.'

'You English, yes?'

'No.'

'Where you from?'

'It doesn't matter.'

'Sanjog adopts a wounded expression. We pass the bloated corpse of a dog on the side of the road. A barefoot boy in rags pokes it with a stick. JD, mindful of being mannerly, answers Sanjog.

'We are from Ireland.'

Sanjog looks confused.

'I-land?'

'Ireland, in Europe... Beside England.'

'Ah England, I know.'

The tuk-tuk scutters to a halt outside a red brick wall. The driver turns to us.

'This is Taj Mahal.'

We disembark and scan a chaotic street. A withered woman pushes a bunch of green bananas into my face as I turn back to the driver.

'Where is Taj Mahal?'

'There,' he says, pointing at a gateway in the red brick. I don't believe him. Surely the Taj Mahal should be visible from the drop-off point. Sanjog beckons for JD to follow him. There are people gathered around the gate. Perhaps the driver is telling the truth. I pull JD back from Sanjog, hand the driver fifty Rupee, tuck my leather whip into my belt and throw my bag over my shoulder. The driver is joined by Sanjog, and they shake heads in unison and wave the fifty Rupee note before my face.

'No, no, my friend, fifty Rupee each.'

I laugh into their faces.

'Twenty-five Rupee each.'

I point to JD.

'Fifty for both of us. No more.'

The driver looks at Sanjog, then back at me. His head bobs from side to side.

'Yes, fifty Rupee for two, but you give me fifty Rupee and him fifty Rupee.'

Sanjog nods vigorously.

'Yes, fifty Rupee for me, I am guide.'

Men gather around and shout across at one another, enjoying the diversion. JD moves closer to me.

'Guide? You're not guide. We don't want guide. I pay for taxi, no more.'

Sanjog, emboldened by the audience, raises his voice as he demands payment for services rendered.

'Go fuck yourself.'

A gasp from the assembled men. Indians consider foul language to be a grave insult. I know this because JD told me so during one of his cultural lessons. The driver takes advantage of his high moral ground to make a speech in Hindi to the assembled masses. He fills them in on the devious westerners who have reneged on a promise to poor innocent Sanjog. Men take turns to tell us to pay our guide. I speak to the driver, loudly and slowly so that all will understand.

'You take me and my friend from train station. I give you fifty Rupee, yes?'

He nods. I point at Sanjog.

'I do not know this man. I do not want guide. I no pay him.'

Sanjog, sensing he is losing the crowd, makes an animated speech and turns back to me, brazen as you like.

'You give me fifty Rupee.'

I stare into his black eyes, move my face close to his.

'No!'

The crowd tighten around us, more out of curiosity than aggression but enough to make me realise we may have to fight our way out of this. The bone handle of a Ghurkha knife juts out from beneath the seat of the tuk-tuk. The driver is between me and the knife. Sanjog is slightly to the left, confident with chin exposed. I can take Sanjog out with a straight left, grab the driver's throat with my right, swing in behind him, grab the Ghurkha knife with my left and use the driver as a shield as we back up into the gate, passing close enough to Sanjog to stamp on his weasel face. I need JD on the same wavelength. If he doesn't stay close, the crowd will swarm over him, and all will be lost. I smile, hold my hands up in resignation, glance to JD.

'You thinking what I'm thinking?'

'Yes, sure it's only a quid. I'll just give it to them.'

I turn to JD and grab him by the shoulders, forcing him to look into my eyes.

'Listen, John, if we have to die right here on the street, we're not giving that fucker fifty Rupees. Are you with me?'

I'm the last person JD wants to be with right now. The colour drains from his face as he realises he is about to die, killed by poor taste in travel companions.

'Please,' he whimpers, 'please.'

He reaches into his pocket, pulls out a fifty, and hands it to Sanjog before I can protest. The crowd disperses as the prospect of further conflict dissipates. Sanjog slinks off down a side street, ignorant to the debt of gratitude he owes my friend.

'C'mon, let's suss out this Taj Mahal.'

'Are you completely insane?'

'What? That's what we're here for.'

JD takes time to gaze at the little scenes sprinkled all around, turns back to me.

'Are you completely insane?'

I'm doing my best not to be angry at him for paying that thieving bastard. Now he's berating me for standing up to the fucker. I walk to the stiles.

We pay one thousand Rupee each, enter through the gates and stand awestruck. All of our hassles and disagreements melt into the ambiance of the enclosed space. Though we are two-hundred metres from the building itself, we know that all the heat and hardship of the past week is vindicated by our arrival into this garden. We sit on a marble ledge at the head of the tree-lined stretch of still reflective water which leads to the marble mausoleum. Parakeets whistle as they flit between trees, flashes of green and scarlet across the blue dome.

JD informs me that the bench we're sitting on is the same one Princess Diana posed upon back in 1992. I feign interest, not wanting to spoil the serenity of the place by telling him how little I care about the deceased princess. It's a mistake. He rabbits on about the irony of her posing alone at this, the greatest monument to love on the planet, then opens his *Lonely Planet* guide and embarks on a historical monologue. The sun is warm on our backs. Floral scents waft through the air with brightly coloured butterflies, and anger slowly seeps out of me, leaving Sanjog a lifetime away, lost somewhere in the stinking grime outside the walls. I watch a tiny gecko bask on sandstone brick as JD speaks.

'The building was constructed by the Mughal Emperor, Shah Jahan, in memory of his wife of seventeen years, Mumtaz Mahal. She died in 1631, giving birth to their fourteenth child. Fuck's sake! Fourteen kids! Catholic blood there somewhere. The heartbroken emperor started building the Taj in the same year, and it took twenty-two years to complete. Workers were brought from all over central Asia, a total of twenty thousand in all. Experts were even recruited from Europe, though the main architect was an Iranian by the name of Isa Khan.'

A tiny middle-aged man, with round spectacles and white robe, approaches. He looks like a re-incarnation of Gandhi himself. He informs us he is a guide and will gladly show us around for a meagre donation. I tell him I have a guide and nod towards JD. He bows politely and leaves. I call him back. The history will sound more authentic coming from Indian lips.

His name is Gurudas, which he informs us means servant of the guru. We descend steps and stroll along the right side of the dividing watercourse on red sandstone paving. His soft voice complements birdsong as a light breeze rises from the Yamuna River. 'You are lucky,' he says, 'morning not busy.' He pauses frequently as we walk, always waiting a few moments before he speaks, as if to absorb the essence of the decorative gardens we pass through. They are set out according to classical Mughal designs, known as *Charbagh*, which consist of a square garden, quartered by watercourses. We stop halfway up, at the *Al-Kawthar*, or 'The Celestial Pool of Abundance', to stand at the dead centre of a cross of mirrored water. Gurudas points to a sandstone building at the end of one watercourse.

'That is museum. We look after, no hurry, enjoy sunshine, yes?'

Gurudas takes deep breaths through his pointed nose, inhaling the ions that rise from the water as the day heats up. I look at the Taj and visualise thousands of workers building as Shah Jahan watches, each marble block reminding him of his great loss as it expressed his undying love. And here it stands, four-hundred and seventy years later. The Mughal Empire long crumbled, British dominion a fading memory, but this beautiful monument to ever-lasting love stands proud and alone in the middle of a shit-hole town, oblivious to the filth, the poverty, the transient eras that come and go through centuries.

JD and Gurudas have ambled up the pathway. I catch up as they climb the steps to the white marble platform that serves as a pedestal for the Taj. Gurudas speaks of the four white minarets that surround the building, one at each corner of the platform. They are purely decorative. The Taj Mahal is not a mosque, so nobody is called to prayer from them. He points out that the minarets lean slightly outwards. This is in case any of them were ever to fall, to ensure they would tumble outwards, so as not to damage the Taj itself. There are identical red sandstone buildings on each side, one of which is a mosque, the other built to maintain perfect symmetry. It cannot be used as a mosque as it faces the wrong direction.

To the rear of the platform, we look out over the Yamuna River and see the Red Fort across the way, an impressive structure even from this distance. The river is low, a glinting silver thread meandering through a flood-plain of sandy marsh, patrolled by platoons of egrets, herons and storks oblivious to the landmarks on either side. As we look across at the fort, Gurudas fills us in on the tragedy of Shah Jahan. He had intended to build a second Taj Mahal, this one in black marble, to be used as his tomb. Plans were drawn up for this perfect counter-image of the white Taj. However, the Shah's son, Aurangzeb, no doubt worried about the steady drain on his inheritance, put a stop to the madness. He overthrew his father and imprisoned him in the Red Fort, where he spent the rest of his days looking out the window of his cell at his wife's tomb.

We curse Aurangzeb for depriving us of a black marble Taj Mahal before walking across the platform towards the main building. JD points to crimson blotches all over the white marble, mementoes of countless paan-chewing Indians. Guradas shakes his head.

'Pigs.'

The central structure is every bit as impressive close-up as from a distance. Perfectly symmetrical, four small domes surround the huge central bulbous dome which crowns perfectly aligned archways containing finely cut marble screens through which light is admitted to the interior. The walls are inlaid with thousands of semi-precious stones arranged in patterns through a process known as *pietra dura*.

The main chamber contains two tombs, which Guradas tells us are false. The authentic tombs – those of Shah Jahan and his wife, Mumtaz Mahal, are in the basement. I'm relieved Aurangzeb at least had the integrity to place his father's remains in an adjoining tomb to his beloved wife. By all accounts, he acted for the good of the empire. Had his grief-stricken father had his way, the family would have been crippled financially. Future tourist revenues would have been scant consolation.

Guradas breaks the sombre hush by howling like a wolf. The sound echoes around the chamber, gaining resonance and timbre as it unfurls and spins along the inside of the dome. We emerge into blinding light, allow our eyes to readjust before walking to the museum. Guradas remains outside while we wander half-heartedly through architectural drawings, Mughal swords and Celadon plates, which JD informs me change colour if poisoned food is placed upon them. We exit to find our guide sitting cross-legged under a tree among the parakeets and starlings. A sacred ibis stands motionless in the shade, its black and white plumage and long orange beak contrasting beautifully with green foliage.

We sit beside Guradas on the grass and watch the garden's activities reflected in the water until our world inverts, and we ourselves become reflections, mere mirror images of an illusion. The sacred ibis disrupts our stupor when it takes flight. We could stay forever, but there is a Red Fort to explore and hunger to be sated. We invite Guradas to accompany us. He declines, tells us he has people to meet, and to only pay twenty Rupee for tuk-tuk. He walks us to the gate. We give him one hundred Rupee for his splendid company and exit to the noise and filth of the outside world. I steal one final glance over my shoulder before being engulfed by touts once again.

We walk up a dusty street, ignore the tuk-tuk drivers, sidestep a shit-covered white cow lying on the baked dirt. We need food. There are a number of restaurants, all decrepit. One to our right has a sign proclaiming: Paradise Restaurant – No 1 restaurant in India. Beside the sign, a black pig roots in the earth with its long snout, grunting with effort. JD takes a photo, proclaiming if there is one definitive image of the region, then this is it.

'Lies and filth, Mont. Lies and filth.'

We head into the Taj Mahal restaurant directly across and are directed to a rooftop terrace. We order two beers and two portions of chicken fried rice. As we drink, we watch an old woman chop wood on the street beneath us. Despite the heat, she is dressed head to toe in black cloth. She wields a short axe like an extension of her right arm, pulling lengths of timber from a large pile to her left, chopping them up and piling the pieces to her right. She pauses sporadically to shoo two mangy goats who eye up the splinters as tasty titbits, coaxing the kindling into a little pile with her feet.

Our meals arrive. Neither of us is surprised to find there's no chicken included with chicken fried rice. The rice is cold and brittle. It requires an incredibly low standard of *haute cuisine* to serve inedible rice. Three chickens strut by on the street below. They scratch the ground, taunting us with succulent breasts. We're past caring. The beers are enough to recharge the batteries for the time being, and the sight of the tiny old woman attacking that gigantic pile of timber with her small axe is enough to put things in perspective. We pay the bill, walk out the door, and jump onto a passing tuk-tuk. 'To the Red Fort, my good man, and don't dawdle.'

The Red Fort is huge, the kind of structure that you fantasise about as a young boy playing war games. We're like children as we wander through the many halls and climb onto the walls. JD proclaims that if he ever becomes a king, he's going to build a fort just like this, from where he can launch attacks on the tuk-tuk armies of the night.

'You can be my general, Mont... all the damsels you can handle.'

I wish Brave Sir John felt as gung-ho a few short hours ago. He reads from his book as we explore.

'Construction of the fort was started by Shah Jahan's grandfather in 1565. The fort at that time was principally a military structure, but by the time our beloved romantic took charge, it had become a palace. The walls stretch for over two point five kilometres and are surrounded by a moat over ten metres wide.'

We browse through the hall of public audiences, pausing to sit on the throne, then on into the hall of private audiences. We find a big hole where they used to chuck prisoners down into the Yamuna back in the day, and we climb the octagonal tower, with its spectacular views over the water to the Taj. This is where the Shah died in 1666, having been imprisoned here for seven years. There is a huge hole in one of the external walls, and we sit with legs dangling and watch the Taj Mahal change colour as the sun slinks across a cloudless sky. I root a spliff from my pocket, the last of our dope. We absorb the view as we smoke, lost in thoughts of empire, love and betrayal.

A tuk-tuk drops us at Taj Road, and we wander stoned into the Kwality Restaurant, hoping the cuisine is of a higher standard than the spelling. It is. We gorge on chicken korma, rice and naan bread, washed down with an ice-cold beer named Golden Peacock. We haven't come across it before, but it passes the Pepsi-challenge. We have another beer and another. After three beers, JD is drunk. I examine the label. Golden Peacock is 7.5% proof. JD slams his glass onto the table, declares this the greatest adventure ever. He's going to continue travelling, a slave to the road from here on in.

'Fuck work, Mont. Fuck it. What thanks do we get?'

We have another beer and another.

The air-conditioned first-class carriage is welcome respite from the fume-smothered platform. I seek out seat forty-two. An Aussie girl sits there beside her companion. She explains that her seat is down the back, but she'd like to be with her friend and asks if I would mind sitting down in sixty-six instead. 'Not at all,' I reply, refreshed by the cool air, drunk on

Golden Peacock. I continue down to the back and slump into the seat. JD sits further up the aisle. He speaks loudly and drunkenly to a girl next to him. I drift off, exhausted after the day.

I'm shook awake. It's JD. He's demented.

'C'mon,' he shouts. 'Quickly.'

A girl to my left, who leaned on my shoulder as she slept, shifts nervously in her seat, disturbed by JD's aggressive manner.

'What's up?'

'C'mon, let's go.'

I look around, bleary-eyed. We're still on the train. It's still moving. All of the passengers have turned in their seats and stare down at JD as he tries to pull me up by the shoulder. The scene has a dream-like quality. I'm not altogether convinced JD is there.

'Come up here a minute.'

Crazed eyes bore into me, sparkling with impatience.

'Up where?'

'Up here with me, we need to sort this out.'

He bristles. Teeth grind like he's overdone it on speed. The people on either side of me move as far away as possible. I grab JD and sit him next to me.

'Calm the fuck down. You're freaking everybody out. What's the story?'

'That fucker up there. See him?'

He points up the carriage. 'That fucker up there' could be any one of twenty men.

'Yeah, you!'

A tanned angular face with blonde hair catches my eye briefly. He turns around and faces straight ahead.

'Jesus, JD, keep it down. Tell me what happened, from the beginning.'

'I'm talking to this girl, Sylvia, right. And her friend comes on and goes to take her seat behind her, but this thick German fucker is sitting there beside his girlfriend, and she asks him to move, like, and he refuses, saying she can have his seat instead.'

'So what? All the seats are fucked up, my seats up there.'

'I know, but she wanted her seat, and Sylvia wanted her to sit there, and they asked him nicely, and still he refused to move. Then I asked him, and he told me to mind my business.'

'What did you say to that?'

'I told him I'd make it my business if he didn't get up and give the girl her seat, and the bollocks just laughed at me, laughed at me, dirty German fucker.'

'Did you do anything?'

'Yes. I came down to get you.'

JD foams at the mouth like a rabid baboon, a monstrous mutation of my normally placid companion. What can have led to this Mr Hyde persona ranting beside me on a night train to New Delhi? The penny drops.

'You take your Larium this morning?'

'What's that got to do with anything?'

'Just checking.'

'We going to sort this fucker out or what?'

'Listen, JD, we can't go dragging him out of his seat in front of everyone.'

'But...'

'Listen. We'll sort it when we reach Delhi, alright? Stay cool for fuck's sake, don't let him know anything's up.'

'We'll sort it?'

'Soon as we arrive. But be cool, don't let on.'

Bloodlust sated by the prospect of retribution, JD gets up and staggers towards the front of the carriage. He throws his German friend a dirty look as he passes, chats to the girls for a moment, and walks back down towards me. He sits two seats ahead on the left. His face appears around the side of the seat like a grotesque glove puppet.

'I gave Sylvia's friend my seat.'

I open my eyes. We have arrived at Delhi. The unmistakable stench of an Indian railway station pours in when the doors open. I remain seated to await JD's move. When the carriage is almost empty, I stand to find him asleep with seat reclined. I gently shake him. It takes him some time to regain consciousness. The disappointment of waking up in India with the mother of all hangovers wrings his face. As we exit the station, he remembers his mission.

'Sylvia. Where's Sylvia? And that German fucker...'

'He ran off the train as soon as we stopped. You gave him a scare, alright.'

'But Sylvia...'

We hang a right towards Arakashan Road and trundle through streets thronged with all manner of man and beast, trying our best to minimise inhalation of the toxic smog. The usual committee of low-life shysters welcome us, but we're too hung-over to even respond with sarcasm. We hurry past the clubbed feet and mutated arms, back to the air-conditioned lobby of the Ajanta Hotel. The odourless cold iced silk on our faces as we enter the building. I'm grateful we went over-budget with this hotel. If there's ever a city to splash out on creature comforts, it's New Delhi.

We're halfway up the stairs when JD stops abruptly, like a man miles from home who remembers he left a deep-fat fryer turned on.

'Ah, for fuck's sake!'

'What's up?'

'We have no dope.'

'We'll sort some tomorrow.'

'I'm dying for a smoke.'

'I'm too tired to go on the hunt. It's too late, anyway.'

'We have to try.'

I'm fed-up of JD's new-found insanity. No more drinking on Larium day.

'Listen, JD, we're both tired and hung-over. Let's go to the room and chill. We'll sort dope tomorrow.'

'I'll go out myself and sort something.'

JD knows I'm not going to let him off looking to score on his own. He has the sense of direction of a newly hatched mayfly and about the same life-expectancy if allowed to wander drunkenly into the perverse embrace of the Indian capital. I talk him into allowing me a shower before we head out again.

The night hits like a clammy putrid towel to render showers a futile gesture. We walk deep into the dank alleys of Old Delhi in the hope of stumbling across a likely suspect. A night bazaar, with stalls selling food, drink and knick-knacks. All open for business, though few people are out and about. We spot a prospect up ahead, on a stool outside a food vendor, sipping chai. He looks the real deal: white, skinny, dreadlocks, dressed in a light cotton robe. If one were to visualise a stereotypical hippie wandering around India in search of enlightenment, the picture would look very much like this guy. We sit down on adjacent stools and order a couple of sprites. It doesn't take long to strike up conversation. Pi is from Dorset and has travelled around the Indian sub-continent for the past two years. Friendly and forthcoming, he's eager to share information and advice with a couple of greenhorns. We manipulate the conversation towards the sacred herb. He warms to the topic and embarks on a mystical sermon through the many strains and variants he's come across on his travels. He weighs up the relative merits of each and nods sagely as he concludes that the best dope is to be found in Kashmir, a two-day hike into Himalayan foothills from a tiny town near the Pakistan border.

'Short, stocky plants carpet the slopes. Gigantic globules of resin glisten in the dawn like diamonds, harvested by Buddhist monks with long suede sleeves before being pressed and rolled on the thighs of young maidens.'

Pi laughs at our rapt expressions.

'Only joking about the maidens. The rest is gospel. You can travel up with me the next time if you'd like. How long are you guys in India?'

We shrug our shoulders, not wanting to let this hardcore traveller know we're only here for a couple of months before we return to our dead-end jobs in the real world. JD's patience runs out.

'Where can we buy this dope?'

'I have some on me.'

JD has never looked so happy.

'I'm afraid I only have enough for a spliff, though'

JD looks like a child who has run downstairs on Christmas morning to find a stocking stuffed with soot. The realisation we've wasted all this time hits him hard. The streets are deserted. There'll be little chance of scoring. I struggle to think of a solution, if only to prevent another psychotic episode. Pi has a proposal.

'I could come back to yours for a smoke. Is it far?'

JD brightens.

'Not far at all, just around the corner actually, air-conditioned room, TV.'

I lay a palm on JD's knee to halt his sales pitch. He'll offer Pi a hand-job next. I have no desire for company, but Pi seems a sound head, and I don't really have a choice.

'Right, c'mon so.'

I lead the way into the maze of darkened laneways. Occasionally we pass a lit doorway and see a child being washed in a basin or men smoking around a black and white Bollywood-spewing TV. Pi asks JD if we know our way. He boasts about my unerring sense of direction. I have no idea where we are. The landmarks memorised are rendered obsolete by the night. I navigate by the paltry remnants of instinct that linger after a long exhausting day. A man shouts at us as he passes on a bicycle. Pi retorts in Hindi before laughing to himself.

'Awful chancers, these Indians.'

A gigantic rat, the largest I've seen so far, steps out of a doorway ten metres ahead and struts up the darkened thoroughfare like an overfed bulldog. I spot a cat further on, preening itself in the light thrown from an open window. The cat looks down towards this inverse Pied Piper scenario, catches sight of the rat, turns tail and runs into the night. It is the most apt metaphor I have come across for this bizarre region.

By chance, we exit onto Arakashan Road.

'Told you he'd find our way back.'

Pi is impressed with the room. He turns on the television 'for the novelty value' and produces the makings from deep within the folds of his hippie attire. I grab cold beers from the fridge, and the three of us drink, Pi on the chair, JD and myself on a bed each. Pi chatters as he skins-up, using about four cigarettes and a colossal amount of squidgy black hash. He speaks of lakes in Kashmir and mountains in Nepal and bodies devoured by vultures at the Zoroastrian temple or burnt on Ghats by the Ganges. JD sits and watches as more and more ingredients are added. He looks anxious anytime Pi pauses at a particularly interesting point in one of his anecdotes. Eventually, Pi holds up a gigantic cone. JD rushes to hand Pi a lighter and watches wide-eyed as the oversized circular tip ignites and glows with the first pull.

A third of the way through the spliff, JD is comatose on his bed. I don't blame him, though resent the fact that I'm the one left listening to Pi, who is outlining the difference, as he understands it, between Theravada and Mayanara Buddhism. I have never been so stoned. He hands me what is still a huge joint and takes a swig from his beer.

'Is your mate alright?'

JD lies motionless with mouth wide open, snow white, beads of sweat sprinkled across his forehead. He looks like a fresh corpse.

'Yeah, he's fine.'

I accept the spliff and take a few baby tokes, not wanting to worsen my condition any more than necessary to keep up appearances. Pi is silent now, watching me. I sense his intentions are malicious. He has the look of a rapist waiting for sedatives to kick in. I glance around casually to scout for a weapon. The room has little to offer. The bedside-lamp may suffice in an emergency if I can grab it in time. There's a small baton stashed in my rucksack.

'You alright, mate?'

'All good.'

I hand him the spliff. He takes a gigantic toke and blows thick smoke rings upwards to be shredded by the ceiling fan. He turns towards the television and Star News.

'Don't know when I last watched TV, nice for a change.'

He settles back in the chair and makes himself comfortable, not a bother on the fucker. I need to get rid of him before I lose consciousness. He turns from the television, appraises my condition.

'That Boris Johnson's a smarmy git.'

I nod agreement, shift on the bed to stay awake, fearful of blacking-out, leaving two of us comatose as Pi helps himself to passports, money and God knows what else. Hairy pervert head on him. I stagger to the bathroom, take off my sweat-soaked T-shirt and splash water onto my face. On the way back, I reach into my rucksack for the baton. I conceal it behind my forearm as I move towards the bed, declining the proffered spliff. Terror distorts Pi's face. He leaps back from me, eyes fixed on the floor to my right. I follow his gaze. There's a long black snake coiled on the floor. I scream, raise the baton to strike the serpent, discover I'm wielding the ornate black leather whip I was conned into buying this morning. I turn to Pi with whip poised. The sight of me, bare-chested with my sex toy, has Pi speechless for the first time since we met. There's no point trying to explain. I'm too stoned.

'Listen, mate, I've got to be going. Thanks for your hospitality. Say goodbye to John for me, alright!'

I lower the whip. Pi shuffles by, traumatised eyes fixed on the studded handle. I drop the whip. He starts, yelps. I extend my hand. He darts to the door, fumbles with the lock, leaves without a backward glance. I sink back onto the bed, and all the effects I kept at bay hit instantly to leave me paralysed on the mattress. I stare up at the fan, feel its breath, hear the soft whirring. The fan coaxes me from my body. I hover, inches from the blades. I look down onto our two bodies, turn and rise through the ceiling, through flickering bedrooms, through the roof, through the thick smog until I float beneath a clear night sky.

I pick out familiar constellations, humbled by the sheer majesty, the immense distances, the boundless possibilities. I think of the millions below, absurd creatures full of self-importance, enraptured by illusions of meaning, a cluster of microscopic mites clinging onto the end of a long thin thread dangling off the vast tapestry of the universe.

Jesus! That's good dope.

Galway City: Christmas Eve 1976

Ma drags out of a fag as she mops.

'What time will Santa come, Ma?'

'Will he have me Action Man, Ma?'

'Are ya sure Santa likes Guinness?'

'UP TA BED TA FUCK OR DERE'LL BE NO SANTA.'

Dat puts deh frighteners on me. I've no notion a sleepin' but figure I'd best play along. Too much 'quiet time' gone into dat Action Man. Up I go and lie with me eyes closed, listenin' for deh tinkle of sleigh bells.

I'm awake, heart pumpin', peepers wide. A thump from deh front room. Dat's Santa down deh chimney I tink and I'm out a deh scratcher. I creep downstairs like a shadow, ease open the door, and dere's Santa, in deh flesh. And he has me Ma by deh head a hair, like, and she on her knees. He yanks her up, smacks her cross deh pus, sends her flyin' into deh tree, knocks deh whole fuckin' ting, like. I dunno wot deh story is. Everybody'd led me ta believe Santa's a sound old skin.

Ma'd hit me a few slaps earlier. Santa must a got wind of it, decided ta teach her a lesson, standin' up for the kids, like. I twig deh blood dribblin' from her mouth, lamp the way she's shakin', cop Santa's lost deh run of himself. He shapes ta hit her again.

'SANTA! STOP!'

Santa swings round quick as lightnin', digs me inta deh kisser.

'BACK UP TA FUCKIN' BED.'

I tumble onto me arse, blood pissin', scramble upstairs through swirlin' stars tinkin' Santa takes dis stay in bed lark fierce serious, hide tremblin' 'neath deh covers, chokin' on tears and snot and blood.

Me auld fella's plonked on deh edge of me bed tellin' me how he arrived home ta find Santa goin' mad, how he dragged Santa outside, warned him never ta return, how he told Santa ta shove his presents, 'cause he knew I wouldn't want dem, not after wot Santa'd done to me Ma. Stinky yellow fingers stroke me burst lip.

'Cause you're a good lad, you.'

Best not ask 'bout me Action Man.

Esmerelda Estevez and the Way She Might Look at You

So I bought myself one of those sex robots. Brenda left me, you see; out of the blue after twelve years, said I bored the tits off her. Clearly a lie. But they do that, the Irish. They tell lies. Call it a 'gift for storytelling'. Then Brenda claimed I'd neglected her, spent my nights upstairs in my man cave watching porn. 'Excuse me', I said. 'It's a study.' No use. Brenda was out the door, into a cab, and that was the last I saw of her.

I turned fifty this year. I don't have the energy to begin a new relationship. Pretend to be a nice guy. A sex robot seemed an ideal solution. I browsed options online. There are a lot of options. AI Angels, a California company, are leaders in the field. Their current generation of sex robots come equipped with an identity – name, nationality, back story and so forth – and their personalities develop as they get to know their 'companions.' After much deliberation, I decided on a brunette named Esmerelda Estevez. God knows why I chose another Irish woman. Perhaps I missed Brenda.

Esmerelda Estevez was top of the range. $8,000 worth of cutting-edge artificial intelligence. I discovered that these high-end models speak with human voices. AI Angels employ porn stars to record the voice-overs, presumably because they're such great actors. The most popular voice is that of

Stormy Daniels. But the voice of Stormy Daniels wouldn't sound authentic coming from the lips of an Irish woman, so I searched the database for a more suitable option. There was only one Irish porn star, and her name was Rainy Day. I inputted the voice of Rainy Day into the online simulator to compare popular phrases side by side with Stormy Daniels. Stormy's southern drawl was soft and soothing.

'Oh my God! You're so big.'

Rainy Day's squawk was wild and feral.

'Jesus Christ all-fuckin'-mighty! You've a bollocks on ya like a Charolais bull.'

Two weeks later, Rainy Day Esmerelda arrived at my front door. I unpacked and assembled her. She was only just gorgeous. I enabled Bluetooth, hooked her up to my phone, inputted the requisite info, and turned her on. Esmerelda's eyes shot open, put the heart crossways in me.

'How's it goin'? I'm Esmerelda.'

'Your eyes. They're so... life like.'

'How's it goin'? I'm Esmerelda.

'I'm Jack.'

'Howya, Jack. Do ya fancy a ride?'

I took Esmerelda by the hand and led her upstairs.

'Jesus, Jack. You've a fine arse on ya.'

For two days and two nights, me and Rainy Day Esmerelda had a wonderful time. And it wasn't just the sex. Esmerelda listened to my stories. Laughed at my jokes. Watched the football. And the way she looked at me, the adoration in those moist hazel eyes, made me feel like I was the only man on Earth.

A few days in, I noticed a slight deviation in tone. On the first couple of nights, Esmerelda had screamed, 'Yeah! Yeah! You're so fuckin' huge!' Whereas on night three, her voice became disinterested, more sneer than declaration, 'Yeah... Yeah... You're *so* fuckin' huge.' And the way she looked at me, as if her adoration had diminished to barely concealed contempt, made me realise my mistake in choosing Rainy Day Esmerelda. Because the Irish aren't just a nation of liars. They're a nation of sarcastic liars. If an Irish person looks at you and says, 'Nice shirt,' it means your shirt looks ridiculous, and everybody's laughing at you. I phoned the manufacturer, demanded I speak to the sales manager.

'Good morning, Mr McGrath. You're through to Megan. How can I help you?'

'Hello, Megan. I wish to return Rainy Day Esmerelda. And I expect a full refund.'

'What seems to be the problem with your model, sir?'

'The way she looks at me for a start.'

'The way she looks at you?'

'And she's developed a sarcastic tone.'

'I'm afraid that's not possible, Mr McGrath.'

'I'm afraid it is possible, Megan. Because it happened.'

'Deviations in tone are not within the capability of the model's processing unit, Mr McGrath.'

'You don't know a lot about the Irish, Megan.'

'Actually, I am Irish, Mr McGrath. My great grandmother is from Tipperary.'

'Yes. You sound Irish.'

'Thank you.'

'You just proved my point, Megan.'

'I'm afraid we are unable to offer a refund in this case, Mr McGrath. You have a nice day.'

Megan hung up. As I stood staring at the phone in my hand, an epiphany shuddered through me. I had a ghost in the machine, and I must destroy Rainy Day Esmerelda before she destroyed what was left of my self-esteem. I turned off Bluetooth, ripped the router from its socket, rummaged through the under-stair cupboard, grabbed a screwdriver and Allen keys from my toolbox, sprinted upstairs and into the bedroom. No sign of Esmerelda. I checked under the bed, in the wardrobe.

'This isn't possible.'

Voices from my study. I crept across the landing and eased open the door. Esmerelda sprawled naked across my recliner watching Pornhub.

'Esmerelda? What are you at?'

'I'm lying here thinking of you.'

'Really?'

'No! Not really. I had to turn myself on. You bore the tits off me.'

The tools dropped to the floor. Too late to save my self-esteem. Too late to save anything.

Eating Swans

Daniel cursed the clear night. The thick fog had lifted, leaving a wispy residue which caught the moonlight and glistened like iced cobwebs over the still water. A swan, he was sure of it, foraged in reeds by the opposite bank. It raised its head, turned, drifted towards the city. Daniel shifted into the short shadows of desolate houses. Concrete blocks ahead, strewn outward in a semi-circle from a U-shaped wound in a garden wall. Daniel crouched among the rubble, watched the swan glide closer. He selected a large block, lifted it two-handed to his chest, staggered briefly, steadied himself, backed slowly along the limestone wall which ran parallel to the canal, matching the pace of the bird. He reached the bridge at New Road, paused to scan the area, hurried over, placed the block by the railing, backtracked to where he could check the swan's position. Almost at the bridge, white plumage stark against the black water as it paddled gently towards its own reflection with wings curled back. Daniel almost lost himself in this vision of a lost world before jolting from the serene grace of the moment.

He scanned roads again as the swan eased beneath the bridge, crossed the walkway, grabbed the block, waited, silhouetted and exposed. The swan failed to emerge. Had it sensed his intention? To survive this long would have taken guile. At least fifteen years since swans graced Galway. Daniel had never seen a live one, at least not that he could remember. His father once told him he'd been attacked by a swan as a child. He was feeding them at the quayside near Nimmo's pier when a cob became agitated and spread giant wings like a vengeful angel to chase a terrified Daniel up the slipway and into the arms of his father. Daniel didn't remember the incident, though he played it in his mind sometimes as he was told it. Daniel didn't believe in angels. He didn't believe in swans either, until he saw this one floating down the canal.

The prospect of cooked flesh shot sharp pangs through Daniel's shrunken stomach. His father's words came to him as he checked the roads again. 'No matter how bad things get, they can always get worse.' The recollection was punctuated by an anguished scream from the direction of the former Garda station at Mill Street. The building served as a base for the Pigs, the tribe that controlled the area around Dominick Street, taking in O'Brien's bridge, Nun's Island and the roadways leading to University Road and the Westside.

A beak emerged a metre to Daniel's right. He pushed the block from his chest, aiming slightly ahead of the swan. The block was arcing off target when the bird, startled by the block's shadow, darted to its left. The concrete struck where the neck curved from the body. A dull gulp, a resonant squawk, cut short as the bird went under. Daniel stood transfixed as the swan struggled from beneath the weight to surface in a thunderous flapping of wings that sent Daniel sprinting for the naked fuchsia bushes further down the left bank. He pushed deep into thin branches, watched the bird attempt to fly. The block had broken its neck. Each time its wings managed to elevate the swan's body, its neck hung limp and its head dragged along the surface until the swan crashed down into the water. The power of the swan's great wings faded as the constant effort to lift itself from the water drained its energy, recent grace replaced by erratic spasms as it stuttered downstream.

One final valiant effort almost took the swan from Daniel. It rose higher out of the water this time, and achieved forward momentum, only to crash heavily into the dilapidated footbridge to the front of the lock. It crumpled, dropped down into the filth and debris trapped by the barrier, life-force seeping into the manky water as it drowned. The night hummed, charged by the recent commotion. Daniel waited. The moon drifted westwards and a breeze rose off the canal. Dark clouds crept from the west and Daniel willed their welcome cloak closer as he shivered in the bushes. Movement caught his eye from down along the path. Dark shapes skulked up the hill behind the Roisin Dubh. Steel glinted as they twisted and turned, ever watchful. Daniel eased into a prone position and lay faced outward, hood pulled over his face. A second group came up the short hill from Henry Street and moved down along the canal. They converged at the lock, thirty metres from Daniel, eleven in total. Daniel recognised the distinctive contours of a face silhouetted in the half-light. The Swans, a tribe based at the Claddagh.

The Swans crept along the canal, stopped directly across from Daniel. A stench of sweat and blood infused the crisp air. A shaven head leaned over railings to inspect the water. The white of the swan was visible from where Daniel lay but obscured to those on the opposite bank. Another two moved to the bridge and crossed. They walked towards him. The taller of the two limped heavily and used a stout blackthorn as a crutch. Its metal tip cracked the ground with each right footfall, beating closer as they scanned the water and sniffed the air. Daniel gripped the handle of his dagger. He would need to get the shorter one in the heart to stand any chance. The tall one was in no condition to give chase. To run for the road would be futile, the tribe would cut him off. He'd head for the footbridge and risk the long drop on the other side of the lock. A short icy swim to the Mill Street bank. Hopefully, the Pigs would not react quickly enough to catch him as he ran through their base, assuming he made it out of the water before it numbed his frail frame.

The two stopped beside him. Daniel kept head down, breathing shallow into dirt, expecting the blackthorn to swing down and crush his skull. Nothing but the rasping breaths of the men. Daniel visualised them looking down at him, nudging one another as they chose blades. He wanted to leap to his feet, take his chances, but cold had stiffened limbs. Sudden dripping onto his back became a steady stream of urine which splashed through branches to spread across his shoulders and run down onto the hard clay. The acrid tang steamed into the threads of mist that clung to the bare fuchsia. Daniel tightened his grip on the hilt, poised to roll outwards and drive the knife into the offender's groin. As he tensed frame and hunched shoulders, vigorous splashing sounded from the canal. The two turned, pointed to the base of the lock, hurried back to the footbridge and crossed to join their comrades. A final spasmodic death throe had betrayed the swan's location and saved Daniel.

The tribe focused on extracting the bird from the water. Two had hook-ended lances but both were too short. The leader snapped at a man to his right, who immediately took a lance from a comrade and lay on his chest. Two took a leg each and lowered him towards the water. It took three attempts to snag the swan. All were silent as it rose slowly towards the bank. A second hooked the bird through the breast when it came within reach. Black shapes eased up and onto the high wall behind the group as a squat bearded man held the swan up by its legs. The bird's head dangled at the end of its long limp neck. Wings fell away from the body to spread wide in one final allusion to its former glory. Two grabbed a wing each and pulled them to their full span. Another pulled the head into his crotch with a manic laugh that was cut short by a spear which entered his mouth to exit through the top of his neck. He crumpled. Men dropped from the high wall swinging and hacking. Two more fell in the brief vacuum between action and reaction as more attackers ran up the incline from Henry Street.

The squat bearded man swung the swan's corpse into the path of an axe-swinging assailant and stabbed low and hard with a short sword. The man ran onto the blade, hunched with a sharp hiss. Bloody froth sprayed over the swan in his arms and he collapsed into a winged embrace that left man and beast entangled breast to breast on the pathway. The leader sliced a passing cheek and called his men to order. The Swans maintained a defensive formation as they retreated down the hill towards the Claddagh.

Battle resumed when they emerged at the crossroads to the front of Monroe's Tavern and the night filled with metallic clangs and hideous cries. Daniel crossed the footbridge and moved to where four bodies lay sprawled. He looked up and down the canal then bent to the first. An axe had left a deep cleave in the centre of the man's forehead. Shards of skull gleamed in bloody mush. Daniel undid the man's trousers, pulled them to his ankles, turned him onto his chest. He took his dagger and cut through the buttocks, three thick slices from each cheek. He took care to avoid the putrid final release congealed behind the scrotum. Black blood seeped upwards then flowed down to glisten the tarmac. The meat over the thighs was next. The blade snagged on tendons but Daniel managed two long slices per leg. He turned the body and harvested thin slivers from the front before spreading the legs to hack at the fleshy bounty around the groin. He placed the dripping cuts of meat into his canvas shoulder bag, breath laboured from the effort.

Engrossed in the second corpse, Daniel heard movement behind. He swung around, crouching as he brought his dagger to bear in a low sweeping motion. A man sat upright, spear shaft protruding from a gaping blood-filled mouth that spluttered blobs towards Daniel. His hands reached for the spear but Daniel grabbed the shaft close to the face. He felt the heat of the man's breath on his knuckles as he levered the head backwards. The man's eyes rolled back into their sockets. Daniel slit the jugular in a smooth backhand motion and put his mouth to the gushing wound. The warmth in his throat made him retch but he persevered, forcing himself to swallow. When he had drunk all he could bear, Daniel sheathed the knife, placed a foot on the man's mangled face, and pulled the spear. He used the spread wings of the swan to wipe bloody mush from its barbed head. Glint of moonlight from the man's left hand. A thick silver Claddagh band, deep blackened indent diagonal across the clasped heart. His father's wedding ring. Daniel left the spear within reach, grabbed an axe from the tarmac, and chopped the finger at its knuckle. He pocketed the ring and repeated the butchering process on the remaining corpses. The sounds of fighting subsided as his bag filled. It would push his luck to stay any longer.

Inky clouds restored darkness to the city of tribes. The bloodied swan lay splayed among the slain. Daniel reached to an outstretched wing, gripped one of the few unblemished feathers, stood on the limb, and pulled hard to pluck the memento. He tucked the single white plume into his waistband, sucked blood from around his teeth, and broke into a gentle jog. The spear rode easy in his right hand and the sodden canvas bag weighed heavy on his shoulder. For the first time in a long time, Daniel felt good about the world.

Uffizi

We stand looking at David, him starkers as the day he was born. I'm disappointed in the size of his penis. I mean, it's flaccid and all but even so, after the way you built him up... I turn to you, say nothing. Look back to David's crotch, curve of your hip snug in my palm, peach blossom fragrant from frizzed hair. A scruff mooches to our side, face smug beneath ragged cream fedora. He too seems unimpressed, tilts head, scratches earlobe. You poke my ribs.

'Isn't he beautiful?'

Penis shatters, balls drop, flat crack pulses through piazza. Another crack: and another. Your chest spews scarlet mist. Clasp you as you slump, swirl from stoneless David. A man-child pans a Kalashnikov. Pilgrims scuttle over cobblestones, dive into archways, drop to join bloodied lumps strewn across the square like one of those Tate Modern installations you drag me to. Mottled fedora flitters through grey gritted air.

Man-child explodes, a brief Goliath. Plinth shatters spine, shards blind. I shudder into a crescendo of crashing waves, peach blossom infused dust of bitter centuries. Flash to you in Boboli Gardens this morning, eyes ablaze as you coaxed a blooming sapling to you and inhaled the world.

De Valera and the Armadillo

On Christmas Eve 1974, my great uncle Malachi arrived home with a randy armadillo and what turned out to be a fatal dose of syphilis. Malachi had been a priest on the missions beyond in Mexico City. I was six at the time and living with my family in a small Connemara farmhouse with no toilet and no running water. We had a piss pot and a plastic basin. I occasionally got the two mixed up. Nothing like a splash of steaming urine to liven a young lad in the morning. We shouldn't have had the piss pot and plastic basin beside one another in fairness, but it was the only free corner in the house. Between grandmother and uncles and aunts and parents and cousins there were twenty-six of us stuffed into a decrepit four-bedroom the size of a half-decent shed. Any who arrived home late in the evening had to sleep standing up. Our cousins in the city worried about contracting polio or tuberculosis. We lived in fear of catching myxomatosis. And that was just the humans in the house. There were dogs and cats and chickens and goats, and now, thanks to my great uncle Malachi, one randy armadillo.

Most everyone was poor in the 1970s, but we were the poor white trash of this poor Connemara village, at least that's what Uncle Malachi called us. When I'd ramble through its boreens as a six-year-old, neighbours in their cow-shit splattered rags would regard me with distain. If I passed within reach, they'd hit me a clip across the ear. You could hit children back then. Even children that didn't belong to you. It didn't matter I'd done nothing wrong. They knew I'd likely do something wrong in the near future, which justified their preemptive strikes. Six years of age and I was being physically abused on a daily basis. Worse than that. I had a severe dose of status anxiety.

Everything changed in the summer of 1975. Malachi died screaming in his bed on Saturday 2 August, and didn't my grandmother discover fifty Irish punts strapped to his waist when she was stripping him down to lay out the body. Once we had Malachi buried, the family convened to discuss how best to invest this windfall. Rather than sort running water or install a toilet, the family decided on the purchase of a colour television, the first colour television in the village.

The news spread like gorse fire. The greatest technological achievement of humanity had arrived in Connemara. And it was sitting above in the front room of our decrepit farmhouse. It no longer mattered that we had no running water. It no longer mattered that we had no toilet. It didn't matter that there was only one channel to choose from. That one channel was in colour. And that one channel broadcast the hurling, and that one channel arrived in time for the All-Ireland hurling semi-final. Galway V Cork from Croke Park, Dublin, on Sunday 19 August 1975.

The day of the match was cruel warm. All the neighbours arrived at our door. The same neighbours who wouldn't doff their caps to us a week before appeared in their Sunday go to mass clothes – men with flat caps in hand, women in their finest frocks, children in their polished shoes and saucepan haircuts – and packed into the sweltering front room until no more could fit. Late arrivals took up positions outside in the sunshine, until they were three-deep looking in the opened front and back windows at the most sophisticated piece of machinery any of them had ever seen. All of us children were put sitting on the floor and told to keep quiet, 'or ye'll get a clip across the ear.' A few pre-emptive strikes were launched by way of warning. I was positioned in the corner by the cabinet and instructed to 'keep an eye on that fucking armadillo.'

Last to arrive was Tom Paraicín, an eighty-five-year-old bachelor from down the hill, 6'5" in his wellingtons, with sidelocks so monstrous, wrens were known to nest in their tangle. For eighty-two of his eighty-five years, Tom Paraicín had survived on a diet made up exclusively of duck eggs and poitín. At least that's what my grandmother told us, and she'd known him all her life. Tom Paraicín positioned himself opposite me, at the doorway into the room. It was the only free space, for good reason, as it was behind the colour television. This didn't bother Tom Paraicín who stared intently at the black plastic back of the device, as happy as if he was sitting in the dugout at Croke Park. And there he remained for the entire match, occasionally glancing away from the black plastic back of the colour television to shout 'Yow' at the array of sweaty faces transfixed by the screen.

Beer, red lemonade and tea were passed around the packed room and out through the windows as we waited for the match to begin. Condensation dripped from the ceiling and ran down the walls. Half-arse Hernan took a swig of Smithwicks and declared it warmer than the tea. As the teams took to the field, commentator, Michael O'Hehir, informed the nation that it was the hottest day in living memory. The room murmured agreement, all except for Tom Paraicín, who claimed to remember a hotter day in July 1945. He didn't elaborate, just took a sip of poitín from a small bottle as cracked as himself and refocused his attention on the black plastic back of the colour television.

Cork were strong favourites according to Michael O'Hehir, having demolished Tipperary in the previous round. Galway hadn't made it to an All-Ireland final since 1958 and hadn't won the All-Ireland since 1928. 'I remember it well,' said Tom Paraicín. 'I don't know can Tom Paraicín remember two minutes ago.' said Slug Flaherty, imitating the lively lilt of Michael O'Hehir. The room exploded in raucous laughter. 'Who's that talking?' asked Tom Paraicín as he scanned the room. His eyes settled on Slug lip-syncing Michael O'Hehir, who didn't feel like today would be the day for Galway. The room screamed abuse at Michael, telling him to 'Shut the fuck up' and 'What do you know, ya bollocks?' I hadn't realised we could communicate with those in Dublin through the colour television. It truly was an amazing piece of technology.

The sliothar was thrown in and all in the room availed of this two-way system, shouting instructions to the players, berating the referee, abusing the Cork players. The scene was the most vibrant and exciting I had witnessed in my six long years on the Earth. Within two minutes, Frank Burke of Galway caught the sliothar, ran twenty yards and stuck it in the Cork net. The room erupted, soaking us in beer and red lemonade and tepid tea. The poor cat, who had been snoozing in the turf basket by the range, sprang four feet towards the ceiling. We'd hardly time to settle when John Connolly scored an even better goal. 'Who are the favourites now, Michael?' Two minutes later, PJ Qualter scored another belter of a goal and pandemonium reigned in our dilapidated farmhouse.

Nine minutes in and Galway were three goals to the good. Men stripped down to their vests in the stifling heat, children to their underwear, women to their bare feet. Michael O'Hehir asked if this could be the day the West awoke from its slumber? The armadillo, who usually slept through the afternoons, began chittering under the cabinet, knocking its amour against the timber base, caught up in the joyous mania which now prevailed.

Cork fought their way back into the match. 'The rebel county has never lost an All-Ireland semi-final,' said Michael, 'It would be a foolish man who'd write them off.' Cork scored a point. Galway scored a point. I could no longer hear the commentary with all the instructions been shouted at the players, who paid little heed from what I could make out. Half-time came and went in a blur, the most memorable sight that of every man and boy in the village lined up pissing side my side in the haggard to the front of the house, all enveloped by a sudden pungent mist which rose to the front of the line. Everybody reassembled in the kitchen and outside the front and back windows. Tom Paraicín reclaimed his spot at the doorway and resumed staring at the black plastic back of the colour television. My grandmother and mother had made a lock of ham sandwiches during the interval and plates passed around the room and out the windows as the sliothar was thrown in for the second half.

Cork hit the ground running, pulled back a couple of points. Galway scored another goal, Cork pulled back two goals, scored three beautiful points from play. They weren't going down without a fight. There was only a point in it as the game went into time added on. Cork drove up the pitch in search of an equaliser, the ball was intercepted, passed down the wing to Connolly, who darted infield and hit the ball high and over the bar just as the referee blew the final whistle. Galway had won the greatest All-Ireland semi-final in living memory. And they'd won it well. And they'd won it in colour.

The room went wild, and the neighbours outside the window went wild, and us children went wild. Dogs barked and howled outside. The goat bleated and leapt into the air. The rooster cock-a-doodled dooed. The armadillo ran out from beneath the cabinet and mounted the cat. The poor cat made an awful commotion but nobody paid it a bit of notice. Tom Paraicín, a man with eighty-five years life experience under his belt, declared it 'The greatest match I've ever seen in my entire life.'

That final whistle didn't just mark the end of a great game of hurling. It marked the end of an era for our family. No longer were we the poor white trash of this poor white village. We were now superior to all. We were sophisticated. We were gentry. We didn't know what social mobility was, but we loved it. Even the pre-emptive strikes ceased. While it was acceptable to hit another man's child. Nobody hit the children of gentry. Thanks to the colour television, I could now walk through the village without fear of assault.

We could hardly wait the three weeks to the final. Galway V Kilkenny in Croke Park on Sunday 7 September. An ideal occasion for us to consolidate our newly elevated status. And then, a tragic opportunity arose. On 29 August 1975, Eamon de Valera died. De Valera was the greatest statesman Ireland had ever seen. He fought in the 1916 Rising, was a leader during the War of Independence. According to my grandmother, he caused the Civil War. He was Taoiseach for about twenty years, and president for fourteen years, only retiring in 1973. Half the country loved De Valera and the other half hated him.

There was no middle ground. We don't do middle ground in Ireland. But love him or hate him, Dev's funeral was going to be the greatest occasion in the history of the Republic. A National Day of Mourning was declared for Sunday 2 September, the day of Dev's state funeral, a funeral which would be televised in full colour. And us with the only colour television in the village.

Preparations were intense and thorough. The house was cleaned top to bottom. The men gathered pallets and built three tier terraces outside the front and back windows. I accompanied my uncle Patsy on an expedition to our cousins in Wormhole to stock up on Poitín. We drew enough spring water from the well to make tea for thousands. And the women made so many ham sandwiches, the pigs would have been justified in declaring their own National Day of Mourning. There was no hosting an Irish funeral without cups of tea and ham sandwiches. We'd be excommunicated. May as well have it without a corpse.

The big day arrived. Two-hundred thousand people lined the streets of Dublin to watch De Valera's funeral cortege make its way from Dublin Castle to Glasnevin Cemetery. Almost as many squeezed into our front room, and when that was full, they gathered four deep on the terraces outside the open windows. Last, but by no means least, Tom Paraicín arrived to take up his usual position at the doorway, and stare intently at the black plastic back of the colour television. We watched in awe as the funeral cortege slowly made its way through the streets of Dublin. Most of those assembled had never seen Dublin, never mind a state funeral, and there was no shortage of observations as we moved through its technicolour streets, army cadets marching ahead of Dev's horse-drawn tricolour-draped casket.

The cortege paused at the Pro Cathedral, and Dev was carried into the church for his final mass, to be celebrated by his grandson. All in the room blessed themselves as the priest took to the altar. The men took off their flat caps and placed them on the floor as mats for their right knees. The women sat where they could, rosary beads wrapped around the joined hands on their laps. After the mass, Dev was hoisted upon the shoulders of cadets, carried out of the church, down the steps and onto the horse drawn carriage once more.

My grandmother and aunts distributed mugs of tea and plates of ham sandwiches as the coffin made its way to Glasnevin cemetery. When the cortege arrived, army cadets, dressed in full regalia, shouldered the tricolour-draped casket to the open grave, and we could all see the green, white and orange of the flag Dev fought for. After the final blessing, Dev's casket was lowered into the grave. The soldiers stood to attention with rifles ready. And we were all glued to it, couldn't believe we were part of history, watching in full colour from a farmhouse in Connemara.

As the soldiers raised their rifles to fire the final volley, a hush descended upon the room. A hush descended on those outside. A hush descended on Tom Paraicín. Even the armadillo stopped licking his parsnip-shaped penis and looked up at the colour television. And didn't my grandmother choose that exact moment to cross the room with a fresh pot of tea. As she passed the colour television, she attempted to look down into De Valera's open grave. And the hushed silence was broken by the clunk of her forehead against the screen. Not only was the silence broken. A spell was broken.

As the rifles shot their final salute over the grave of Ireland's greatest statesman. Our neighbours clamoured down from the terraces outside the windows. Our neighbours hurried out of our front room. They all strode purposefully down the hill away from our house, seemingly ashamed of having ever darkened our door. I ran outside, not understanding what had just happened. The last to leave was Tom Paraicín, a man of eighty-five years life experience. He paused beside me for a moment and watched the village walk away. He looked down at me. 'Jesus, a mac,' he said, 'that was the greatest match I've ever seen in my entire life.' He raised his hand and hit me a clip across the ear. And then, I understood. With the clunk of my grandmother's forehead against the colour television, our neighbours all had the same realisation. These people aren't gentry. These people aren't sophisticated. They're just poor white trash with a colour television. Pre-emptive strikes had returned.

Visitation

A mink startled me earlier by knocking on our patio door. Upright on its hind legs, indignant eyes peering in, wedding ring clack of its claws on the glass. For a brief illogical moment, I thought it was you, returned to assure me that you're still about, watching over me. I was in that half-wakeful state that facilitates such fancies. Perhaps it was his little grey beard, his cocky demeanour, the tilt of his head. Let's just say, in my defence, there was a resemblance.

You didn't believe in an afterlife. Yet here I sit, scrolling through yours. Friends wish you a happy birthday. Women I've never heard of express their love with flurries of emojis, post photos from festivals, clubs, wild parties. Swap anecdotes. Moments shared in your other lifetimes. Is it weird to be jealous of people I've never met?

Mr Mink had obviously wandered up from the canal, spotted his reflection, and enjoyed a narcissistic interlude in his routine. I walked out onto the towpath after he dropped from the glass, watched his sleek figure amble away. He stopped at the lock, stared back at me, brazen as you like, then slid into the brown water with barely a ripple.

I'm jealous of their grief. Its communality. I want to post Happy Birthday, with love-heart emoji, the short poem I wrote for you. Silly, I know. Narcissistic as Mr Mink. It would feel like a betrayal, somehow, given there's no trace of me, of us, in this compilation of your greatest hits. Does grief require acknowledgement to be validated?

I suppose an online afterlife is logical as any version of the concept. Contact has become virtual for the living, just as for the dead. Ironic, given you hated social media. Your most recent post, 364 days ago.

'Thanks for the birthday wishes. Survived the cull for another year.'

I switch to my newsfeed. 'Millions of Minks Culled in Denmark.' They've got the virus apparently, transmitting to humans. There'll be a Europe-wide slaughter. Is it wrong that this news pleases me?

Kind of Blue

Ghosting along damp, deserted streets in the pre-dawn gloom, cherry blossoms confetti beneath my feet. Mute trumpet keens from an open second-floor window. *Flamenco Sketches.* A slender woman silhouettes in soft backlight swaying to Coltrane's tenor saxophone. I stop. Sip of her solitude. Two of us alone together. Tune washing through my veins like primo junk.

Movement ahead. A fox freezes in the act of crossing. Leaves rustle castanets above our heads. Neither of us should be here, yet here we are, skirting the shadows of this toxic city, demonised by the tortured multitudes who will monitor through locked down panes from daybreak. We will be out of sight by then. Curled deep into forgotten crevices. Away from the hostile glance. The accusatory glare.

But for now, I will dance slow upon drenched petals. Breathe deep of the rain-rinsed breeze. Dream my way to The Church at that moment when the stars aligned and those cats surrendered to the notes and chords and beats and broke free. Free to lose their selves in the collective. Free to find the collective in their selves. Free to distil the pungent mash of the past into one pure present.

One take. Those cats nailed it in one take.

All Roads Lead to Ballinasloe

I was four days into a meth binge, shooting pool with a one-legged dwarf in The Village Idiot on West 14th Street. The dwarf's name was Rosie. She turned tricks on 8th Avenue and hustled when business was slow. Rosie smelt of sandalwood and carried a blackthorn shillelagh which served as both walking aid and weapon. I was down sixty bucks, but it was worth it to watch her drag a beer crate round so she could shillelagh-vault up and shoot with her sawn-off cue. 'No tricks tonight?' I asked as I handed over another twenty. 'Not tonight, Three-Piece,' she said. 'Never did find no man wanted to ring in the new year with a one-legged dwarf.' 'Well, you found one now,' I said. 'Rack them up. Double or nothing.'

Hatchet and Olivia, my binge buddies, snorted a couple of key bumps and paid four dollars at the bar for two pints of goldfish. They fed the goldfish to the piranha, laughing maniacally each time they dropped one into the large turbulent tank by the front door. When out of goldfish, they perched on two stools, watched me and Rosie shoot pool, slammed tequilas, and squawked indecipherable instructions over Johnny Cash. A bunch of bikers had 'San Quentin' on repeat. They necked Budweiser and arm wrestled as they sang along at the far end of the long narrow room. One shouldered me on his way to the bar, swung his bearded belligerence into my face. 'You ever do time in San Quentin?' he asked. 'You ever do time in Ballinasloe?' I answered and potted a solid. The biker stood in silent contemplation for some time, as if what I had said was incredibly profound. Perhaps it was. Who knew what passed for profound in The Village Idiot?

The evening was haunted by the lost souls of downtown. Hookers and shysters seeking respite from the bitter wind. Dealers blowing off steam after the last-minute rush. Loners worn down by solitude. All of us chancers at the last chance saloon. Towards midnight, we became aware of a suited man circling the room. He had an uptown look about him. Tailored threads and slicked-back hair. Feigned nonchalance diminished with each lap, his face gradually assuming the demeanour of a man being stalked by a malevolent spirit. Rosie eased up beside him and grabbed his hand. He turned to find nobody there and screamed. Rosie yanked his tie until he spotted her below. 'You looking for a good time, honey?'

Rosie had just sucked helium from one of the disinterested balloons which languished against the black ceiling. The man crumpled to his knees and burst into tears. Rosie pulled his face into her breasts, cackled a high-pitched cackle, and shimmied into him. 'I can't leave,' he cried, when she let him breathe. 'I can't find the door.' One of the bikers put 'Hotel California' on the jukebox, and everybody in the room sang along and danced a clumsy jig around the fallen man as he descended deeper and deeper into horrific psychosis. On the third repeat of the track, I decided enough was enough and pulled the blubbering man-child to his feet. I led him through to the front bar, past the dominatrix whipping the bare arse of a moustached man, past the feeding frenzy in the piranha tank, past the cigar-chomping Latina bargirl and into the night.

The man gulped deep of the icy air, shot glances up and down the deserted street. I placed a hand on his shoulder. 'This isn't your world, my friend.' He looked up to where the neon sign blinked 'ILL ID'. 'I took a wrong turn.' 'We all take wrong turns,' I said. 'Those fiends in there just kept taking them.' He quietened. Settled into a pensive vibe. No doubt attempting to imagine what succession of wrong turns could lead to a place like The Village Idiot on New Year's Eve. The experience had broken something inside of him, shredded his uptown shield. He would never again strut through the doors of an unassuming bar on an unassuming street, would always fear the falsetto amputee dwarfs, the choral bikers, the ravenous piranha that lurked within.

A cab swung into the street from 7th Avenue. I waved it down and bundled the man into the back seat, threw the cabbie a twenty and told him to bring the man uptown. The man pressed his face to the window and stared at me until the cab crossed 8th Avenue. I followed its taillights until it turned right onto 9th before walking back into the bar. The stench of weed, whiskey, poppers, and stale beer hit like a damp putrid cloth after the night air. Rosie dished out tequilas she had bought with the cash from the man's wallet. 'I'm owed twenty.' I said. 'I'll play you for it, honey.' 'Okay. Rack them up.' It was almost midnight. The bikers chose 'Life in the Fast Lane' to ring in the new year. We threw back shots and sang along as Rosie did backflips around the room, pogoing off her one leg like a crazed munchkin. We had counted down to one when Rosie misjudged a flip and cracked her head off the pool table. Olivia screeched, 'Tonight we're going to party like it's

1999,' her meth-mangled face towards the ceiling. The rest of us gathered around an unconscious Rosie, looking down on her as we would at a deformed new-born, none of us knowing quite what to say.

Alicia came out from behind the bar and joined our circle, exhaled a plume of cigar smoke onto the prone dwarf. 'She dead?' I hunkered down and placed two fingers on Rosie's sweaty neck. 'No,' I said, and rolled Rosie face down. Her scalp was cut, but the bleeding wasn't serious. 'Anybody got any medical training?' I asked. 'Gruff is a doctor.' said one of the bikers, pointing at the man who had shouldered me. 'You a doctor, Gruff?' 'Yeah,' he said. 'What kind of doctor are you?' 'Philosophy. I have a PhD from Berkeley.' 'Thank God for that. If there is one,' said Hatchet, and laughed himself into a coughing fit. Olivia lurched forward and handed me a wrap. 'What's that for?' 'To wake her up. Blow some meth up her nose.' 'Maybe we should call an ambulance,' said Gruff. 'Fuck that,' said Alicia. 'An ambulance means cops.' 'Fuck that,' we all agreed.

Me and Hatchet hoisted Rosie onto the pool table. Alicia fetched a thick straw from behind the bar, snipped it in two with her cigar cutter and handed it to me. I stuffed a bump of meth into the straw with my bank card, crushed it on the edge of the table, inserted the straw into Rosie's left nostril and blew hard. We all stood around the pool table and watched, the first silence of the night. Hatchet grabbed Rosie's wrist and counted down seconds on an imaginary watch. Olivia mounted the pool table, squinted down at Rosie's cherub face. Thirty seconds later, Rosie's eyes shot open and she lurched upwards like a woman defibrillated, knocking Olivia off the table. 'Muthafucka.' Rosie glared at us, snorting through flared nostrils. Olivia scrambled to her feet, skirt hitched up her spindly legs, right side of her face caked in grime from the manky carpet. She nodded at me as if she had just successfully tested a cure for cancer. Gruff and Hatchet hoisted Rosie off the pool table and placed her on her foot. She stood swaying, scanning the room with lemur eyes until she located her blackthorn shillelagh to one side of the pool table. She hopped around the table, retrieved her stick, and turned to the bikers. 'Which one of you muthafuckas dry-gulched me?' Rosie vaulted forward and cracked the skull of the nearest biker, a monstrosity with a confederate flag tattooed just below his neckline. He slumped onto the floor, taking out two tables as he fell. Gruff ducked the next swipe. The rest scattered. Rosie pursued them around the room swinging her shillelagh with each hop, bottles and glasses smashing in her wake. Olivia fled into the front bar, horrified at the monster created by her meth experiment. I collapsed next to Hatchet in a corner, both of us incapacitated by hysterical laughter. Alicia sidled along the wall and stood over us. 'Get that crazy bitch outta here. *Ahora!*'

I grabbed Rosie from behind. Hatchet snatched her shillelagh and between us, we wrestled Rosie out the door and into the sub-minus smog which now filled the streets and avenues. I was struggling to position Rosie so she couldn't kick back into my balls when Gruff emerged from the bar and grabbed my arm. 'Tell me, man. How bad was Ballinasloe?' I tightened my hold on the crazed one-legged dwarf in my arms and looked him dead in the eye. 'Honestly? Makes this place look like kindergarten.' Gruff watched after us as we dragged Rosie into the thick fog, lost in imaginings of Ballinasloe, thanking the biker Gods he never did time there.

We got Rosie back to our ramshackle two-bed on Bleeker Street, threw three benzos into her and sat on her until she passed out. The apartment was freezing. Olivia stomped around, pissed because she needed a shower and there was no hot water. We assured her we'd sort it and stumbled down into the basement. Hatchet smacked himself on the forehead as we approached the boiler. 'Fuck's sake. The oil. We forgot the fucking oil.' The two of us had been on our way to order heating oil when we scored the meth. We sat by the parched boiler and smoked a spliff. 'No chance of sorting any today,' I said. Hatchet toked deep, exhaled a succession of pungent rings towards the cladded ceiling. 'Yeah. Well, we have to think of something. Olivia'll go fucking ga ga if there's no heat.' We snorted a couple of bumps to kickstart our stalled brains. Hatchet leapt to his feet. 'I have a plan,' he said, and bolted up the stairs.

Olivia swung towards me as I entered the room. 'Disney World, Three-Piece. Hatchet's bringing us to Disney World.' I look to Hatchet. 'Disney World? Florida?' 'No. Disney World, Alabama. Course it's Florida, dipshit.' Olivia jumped up and down, clapping her hands. 'It's New Year's Eve every night at Disney World. Did you know that, Three-Piece?' 'There's no way we'll be allowed onto a flight in this state.' I said. 'You two need to look in a mirror.' 'We're driving,' said Hatchet. 'Driving? It's a thousand miles. We haven't slept in four days.' 'We can do one more day,' he said, as if days were served in shot glasses. 'We have half an ounce of meth, a bag of weed, a tank full of gas.' 'We're not the fucking Blues Brothers.' I shouted, hoping my raised voice would puncture the fantasy. Olivia cracked into deranged laughter, ghoulish with her pallid dirt-caked face and gigantic pupils. 'It's a twenty-four-hour drive.' I said, lowering my voice this time so my pitch for sanity might seem credible. Hatchet consulted his wrist. 'We can do it in twenty.' He consulted his wrist once more. 'I reckon we do five four-hour shifts between us.' 'And what if we get pulled over?' 'It'll be fine. I'm sober.' 'Yeah, he's sober. You're a fucking buzz kill, Three-Piece.' 'What about Rosie? We can't just leave her here.' 'We'll take her with us,' said Hatchet. 'Yeah, we'll take her home, man.' 'Olivia, Rosie lives in Brooklyn.' 'She lives in Brooklyn, but she's from Disney World. All dwarfs are from Disney World, man.' Olivia looked to Hatchet, exasperated by my ignorance. 'Hatchet,' I said, 'will you tell her, or will I?' 'She's right. It'll be good to have Rosie in the car if we get pulled over. We can tell the cops we're returning a dwarf to Disney World. Nobody's going to fuck with Disney World. They'll just wave us on.' It was futile to argue against this logic. We were driving to Florida.

We gathered drugs, cash, clothes and Rosie's shillelagh. We were unable to rouse Rosie, and didn't want to risk the meth remedy, so I rolled her in a duvet, slung her over my shoulder and carried her to the parking garage. When we arrived at Hatchet's battered Chevrolet Impala, Olivia refused to share the back seat with Rosie. 'I look like fucking Snow White to you? That crazy bitch freaks me out.' The security guard stepped out of his kiosk when he heard the commotion. I asked Hatchet to pop the trunk and placed Rosie inside. Hatchet threw the security guard a twenty as we reached the exit. 'It's okay,' he shouted, 'we're returning a dwarf to Disney World. Happy New Year.' We screeched out of the parking garage, turned right onto 12th Avenue, took the Lincoln Tunnel to New Jersey and headed south on the turnpike. I put a Digweed Ibiza mix on at full volume and sparked up a spliff. 'This is great', said Hatchet. 'Best idea ever.'

We drove south, passing Philly, Baltimore, DC, into Maryland, sticking to four-hour shifts, one driving, one navigating. We took a pitstop every changeover and did a key bump every thirty minutes. It took two hours to convince Olivia to drop a benzo, another hour for it to kick in. The resultant tranquillity was bliss. We switched the soundtrack to Miles Davis and floated through Virginia, into North Carolina as dusk cast long shadows over the landscape. We'd just pulled out of a truck stop outside of Fayetteville when Hatchet checked the rear-view mirror. 'Shades.' I turned around to see a Highway Patrol car riding our tail. 'Will we make a run for it?' asked Hatchet, his tone that of a man suggesting a scenic shortcut. 'Make a run for it? Where the fuck will we run to? Play it cool, for fuck's sake.' 'I'm cool as Fonzy,' said Hatchet, 'I'll just tell them we're bringing a dwarf back to Disney World.' 'Jesus, we forgot about Rosie. How long has she been in the trunk?' Hatchet consulted his wrist. 'Not long. She'll be fine.' 'Not long? It's been about twelve fucking hours. She's probably dead.' 'Let's hope not. She's our ticket out of here if these pig fucks pull us over.' 'Don't tell them about Rosie.' 'Why the fuck not?' 'They hate dwarves, down here.' 'I thought it was blacks they hated.' 'They hate dwarves as well.' 'What about black dwarves?' 'They have no chance.'

Hatchet shook his head and whistled, taken aback by the prejudice prevalent in these here parts. He turned to me, eyes bulging, face gaunt in the half-light. 'Grab Olivia's handbag.' 'You want to powder your nose or something?' 'Perfume, dipshit. Need to clear the stench of weed.' I reached back and plucked Olivia's handbag from her lap. Sirens and flashing lights behind as I rummaged through it and retrieved a bottle of *eau de cologne*. 'Fucking cannabis scented. What kind of crazy bitch has cannabis scented *eau de cologne*?' 'She's quite the ticket,' said Hatchet and sniggered. 'I'll open the windows.' He hit the switch. Smoke billowed from both sides of the car as Hatchet pulled up on the shoulder. The squad car swung in behind. Its flashing lights scorched our dehydrated eyeballs. A torch-bearing officer waddled alongside the car; free hand poised over his sidearm. A bloated midriff filled the window before a flushed face peered in, torch beam resting briefly on an unconscious Olivia before settling on the handbag on my knees. Modus operandi: abduction.

'How's it goin', officer?' chirped Hatchet, his elbow out the window, a man shooting the breeze with an old friend. 'Y'all Irish?' asked a nasal drawl. 'We sure are,' said Hatchet. 'Well, ain't that a doozy? I'm Irish. Where y'all from?' 'Galway.' 'Well, ain't that a doozy? My folks are from Galway. My Granddaddy was John Keady from Ballinasloe. You folks know Ballinasloe?' 'Yeah. We both spent time there.' 'Y'all don't mean the loony bin, I hope.' The three of us laughed long and hard, Hatchet slapped the steering wheel, overcome with mirth. 'Wouldn't that be a doozy?' asked the officer when our laughter subsided. 'I know the Keadys.' said Hatchet. 'Good hurlers.' 'You know the Keadys? Well, ain't that a doozy?' 'I'll tell them you said hello.' 'I sure would appreciate that. You tell them John Michael Patrick Keady says howdy. Y'all driving from Boston?' 'New York. Ran out of heating oil. Decided to head south to Orlando. See Disney World.' Officer John Michael Patrick Keady guffawed long and hard. He bent over and poked his swollen head into the car, into the stench of weed, above the white powder sprinkled across Hatchet's crotch. His voice lowered to a whisper. 'Y'all aware that there's no firearms in Disney World?' 'No,' I answered. I didn't know that.' He turns his face towards Hatchet, close enough to kiss. 'Not even security. Now, ain't that a doozy?' 'That sure is a doozy,' I said, hoping to draw his attention from Hatchet, who was liable to bite the nose off John Michael Patrick's flushed face if he didn't pull back. 'Especially with those dwarves on the loose.' That drew his attention alright. I had no intention of bringing dwarves into the conversation. The words left my mouth before I could spot them and rein them in. John Michael Patrick stared at me. 'We don't take to dwarves round these here parts.' Hatchet nodded. 'Can't be trusted.' 'That ain't maybe,' said John Michael Patrick. 'Shoot you quick as look at you.' He looked at each of us in turn before extracting his head from the car. He straightened up and slapped the roof. 'You folks have a safe journey now, you hear?' Thanks, officer. We'll be sure to say hello to the Keadys.' 'I'd sure appreciate that.' He waddled back to his patrol car. It pulled out and headed down the highway, lights flashing. We watched it speed away. 'Fuck me.' said Hatchet. 'How weird was that?' 'What the fuck's a doozy?' I asked. 'Fucked if I know.' Hatchet consults his imaginary watch. 'We'll have to make up time. Fancy a bump?'

It was past 3a.m. when we pulled into a Days Inn motel on International Drive. We flopped out of the car, mangled. The air was a crisp summer night cool. Frogs whirred nearby, and the champagne perfume of magnolia infused the faint breeze. We each did a bump to straighten ourselves out. I checked us in to adjacent rooms while Hatchet attempted to rouse Olivia. When I arrived back with the key cards, Olivia was sitting on the bonnet, face on her like a bag of Gurkha knives. 'What the fuck are we doing in Orlando?' 'We're going to Disney World,' answered Hatchet. 'Fuck Disney World. Who the fuck wants to go to Disney World?' I handed Hatchet their key cards. 'Our rooms are around the back, ground floor.'

Hatchet popped the trunk so we could grab our bags. Rosie lay face up, eyes shut, mouth agape, neck crisscrossed with dried spittle. 'Rosie. We forgot Rosie. She's fucking dead.' Hatchet checked his imaginary watch. 'She's fine.' I placed my hand on her neck. Warm. With a pulse. Olivia slapped Hatchet across the face. 'You fucking Rosie, you piece of shit?' Hatchet and Olivia clawed at one another while I plucked Rosie from the trunk and threw her over my shoulder. I grabbed my bag and her shillelagh and headed across the parking lot. 'I'm going to bed. See you two in a few hours.'

A heated outdoor pool lay steaming about twenty metres from our rooms. At its edge, a blue heron stood one-legged, gazing into the up-lit water. I opened the door, laid Rosie on one of the beds and skinned up with trembling hands. I was jittery, wracked with shakes and spasms. Hatchet and Olivia burst into the adjacent room, screaming at one another. I needed sleep but couldn't take a benzo until Rosie woke. If she came to in an Orlando motel with me unconscious on the bed, there was a good chance she'd beat me to death with her shillelagh. Thumps from next door as Oliva threw shit at Hatchet. I decided on a night swim. Anything to get away from the madness, work the meth out of my system.

I'd forgotten to bring trunks so stripped naked and eased into the pool's warm embrace, the water silk on my skin as I swam slow lengths under the watchful eye of the heron. The jitters slowly dissipated as I swam, turning onto my back occasionally to gaze at the clear night sky, the indifferent stars, the clumped pointed leaves of the orange trees which lined one side of the pool. I emerged refreshed into the cool air, sat on a sun lounger to dry off, and sparked up. I was kicked back, naked, spliff in hand, when a gigantic pick-up truck screeched into the car park, mounted the kerb, demolished a sapling, and skidded to a halt about four inches from my bare feet. A Latino man leapt from the driver's seat, slammed the door, and headed towards the motel. 'Hey, asshole!' He swung around, glowered at me over the pistol in his right hand. A naked Irishman stretched out smoking a spiff on a cold winter night was obviously not something he had allowed for when he visualised his arrival at the motel. He was hyped on something. Epileptic eyes struggled to relay the scene to his brain. His face twitched with the effort.

I slowly brought the spliff to my lips and toked, allowing him time to settle. His deranged glare followed the spliff, strayed to my crotch. The cold wasn't doing me any favours. 'You mind not pointing that hand cannon at my face?' 'Who the fuck are you?' 'Who the fuck are you? You nearly ran me over, you gomey.' 'What are you doing out here? In this cold?' 'I don't feel the cold.' 'You Irish?' 'Yeah. You want a hit?' I stand. He lowers the gun and accepts the spliff. I grab my towel and wrap it around my waist. 'I'm Three-Piece.' 'Jesús.' He takes a hit. 'What you doing chilling out here, bro?' 'My friend and his girl were fighting. Brain was fried... You planning to shoot someone with that thing?' 'My fiancé.' 'That might spoil the wedding.' 'There ain't gonna be no wedding, bro.' He hands over the spliff, slumps onto the end of my sun-lounger. 'She up there with another man?' 'My friend.' 'He ain't no friend,' I said. Jesús contemplated a small lizard at his feet for a moment before nodding. 'And she ain't no fiancé,' I continued, 'not anymore.' Tears splashed onto the tiles, startling the lizard. It darted beneath a shrub. I fumbled into my clothes. The lizard emerged, tentative, tongue-flicked a teardrop.

'So, you're going to do a life sentence for a woman who's not your fiancé and a man who's not your friend?' 'Who says

I'll get caught?' 'Your pick up's on camera entering the car park at high speed. There's cameras outside the rooms. We're probably on camera right now, you with a gun in your hand.' He stares at the gun, thumb shifting the safety. 'Listen, I'm not saying not to kill those two fucks, maybe they got it coming. I'm saying that you serving life without parole defeats the purpose. Why should you lose your life?' 'Maybe I don't care, bro.' 'You'll care. When that door slams shut behind you, you'll care.' He slipped the safety off, pointed the gun at his face, peered into the barrel. Tears plopped onto the gun, trickled onto a trembling hand. 'Not to mention the fact you'll be deaf.' He lowered the gun, turned to me. 'You ever shoot a .357 in an enclosed space?' Jesús shakes his head. 'That thing'll blow out your eardrums, man. You'll be deaf for weeks. Those pieces are for movies, or warzones, or rednecks on shooting ranges with ear protectors and polaroid glasses who imagine they're blasting away at *hombres*. No offence.' 'None taken.' 'And they kick like a riled jack ass. You'd probably fire a round and drop the fucking thing.'

He held the gun at arm's length, panned along the top of the border hedge. 'All I'm saying is, that gun's the wrong tool for this particular job.' 'You know a lot about firearms?' 'I know enough.' 'Where'd you do time?' 'Ballinasloe.' 'Where's Ballinasloe?' 'In another lifetime.' Jesús placed the gun on the lounger, put his face in his hands, wiped his tears. 'What the fuck are you, bro? A leprechaun or some shit?' 'I'm no leprechaun. I have one in my room, though.' 'Now you're fucking with me.' I placed a hand on his shoulder. 'You know a place where we can get a beer?' 'Yeah. I know a place.' 'Does it have a pool table?' 'Yeah. It has a pool table.' 'How about we do a deal. Give me five minutes to run to my room and change my clothes, and if I come back here with a leprechaun, we'll all go for a beer and forget about shooting those two fucks.' 'How do I know you won't call the cops?' Do I look like somebody who's going to call the cops?' Jesús eyed me up and down. 'You look worse than I do, bro.' 'Yeah, it's been a long day.' I grabbed towel and shoes and made for the room. Jesús hissed. I turned to face him. 'Hey bro. You believe in fate?' 'Do I fuck.' Jesús smiled. A gigantic wide-ass smile that shone luminescent in the pre-dawn gloom.

There was no smile on Rosie when I entered the room to find her hopping from the ensuite wrapped in a white towel. The TV was on, an advert for the local Ripley's Believe It or Not! museum. She grabbed her shillelagh. 'Three-Piece, you muthafucka. What the fuck am I doing in Orlando? And why's my head split like a cantaloupe?' 'Long story.' 'Yeah, well it better be one kicking muthafucka of a story.' Rosie hopped towards me with shillelagh raised. The towel fell from her as she backed me into a corner. I maintained eye contact. 'You up for a hussle?' 'What the fuck you talking about?' 'I found a place. Easy pickings.' 'It's near five a.m.' 'I've a friend waiting outside. He'll drive us there.' Rosie shapes to strike. 'You lying muthafucka. You ain't got no friend outside.' Seriously. My friend, Jesús. He's waiting in the parking lot. C'mon. Let's go shoot some pool.' She relaxed her grip, lowered the shillelagh. Her right breast flopped down as she did so. 'Would you mind not staring at my tits?' 'I wasn't.' 'I'm looking at you.' 'I am now. Cause you brought attention to them. Listen, Jesús is in a hurry. We can discuss breast etiquette when we get to the bar.' 'You got any meth?'

Jesús couldn't have looked more shocked if I'd walked out hand in wing with an ostrich. He stared at Rosie after I hoisted her into the middle seat. 'What the fuck are you gawking at?' 'Jesús, this is Rosie.' 'You weren't shitting me, bro.' 'No. I wasn't shitting you. Let's go have that beer.' We mounted two curbs and knocked a 'Drive Slowly' sign before exiting onto International Drive. I lost count of the number of times Rosie screamed 'Muthafucka' as we swerved through traffic, past lines of motels, diners and tourist tack. Jesús pointed out minor attractions, speaking in a soft rhythm so at odds with his driving I became convinced we'd been killed instantly in a head on collision and were now in an ever-recurring loop where a psychotic saviour informs us that Wet and Wild is indeed wet and wild again and again until the end of time.

Jesús swung into a small unlit parking lot. Aside from a line of Harleys, the lot was deserted. As we pulled up to one side of the motorcycles a bulky figure emerged from the shadows holding what looked to be a sawn-off shotgun. Jesús greeted him with a chirpy 'Hey bro' as he leapt from the cab but obviously wasn't worthy of a response. I swung Rosie down from her seat and followed Jesús to a steel door set between two barred windows. An acrid stench seeped from garbage skips lined along the walls on either side. Jesús rapped on the door, smiled at me like a man who had just brought us to an exclusive Oscars afterparty in Beverly Hills. A narrow shutter slid back at eye height, clunked shut. Rosie poked me. 'I feel like we're in a Scorsese movie. About to get whacked' 'It's cool,' I said. 'Trust me.' 'Trust you? Last time I had a drink with you I woke up a thousand miles away in a fucking motel room.' 'I told you. There's a perfectly reasonable explanation for that.' 'Yeah? I can't wait to hear that story.' The door opened into a narrow hallway lit by a single red bulb. 'Smoke on the Water' blared from within. Jesús led us past a bearded doorman, through a musty corridor with storerooms on either side, into a long windowless room with two pool tables at the far end. High-back booths lined one wall, facing a bar counter, along which stagnated a spangled selection of drooped loners watching reruns of the weekend's basketball on mute. In one booth, three cackling sex workers sat around an overflowing ashtray, downing shots. In the next, a rugged bald man in combat fatigues nursed a beer as he watched the room. Two booths up, a bag lady ate yoghurt with a plastic fork. A bunch of bikers with Banditos patches were shooting pool. A pungent cloud of marijuana smoke clung to a low ceiling, hazing the room. 'Three-Piece, you Muthafucka. You found The Village Idiot of Orlando.' 'Told you to trust me.' 'Fuck you. Bring me a tequila.' Rosie pogoed over to the pool tables, hyped on the line of meth she'd snorted back in the room. It was almost worth the thousand-mile drive to see the facial expressions of the Banditos when Rosie slapped a dollar bill marker on a table.

A bartender appeared from below the counter as I approached, a lithe Latina woman with collagen lips and a flattened nose. '*Hola*. Four shots of tequila in a Slim Jim with two cubes of ice and a slice of lime. And two beers.' 'What kind of beer?' I pointed to where Jesús was chatting to the man who had let us in. 'Whatever Jesús drinks.' Two frosted bottles of Corona were plucked from a cooler and placed on two paper napkins. She twisted the caps off before scooping two cubes of ice into a Slim Jim, adding a chunk of lime and free pouring the Tequila. I threw thirty bucks onto the counter and brought the tequila down to Rosie. The baiting was well underway. One Bandito told a brother to forfeit his turn and 'Let the little lady shoot.' 'Who the fuck you calling little lady you hairy piece of shit? I ain't no fucking lady.' The Banditos were laughing as I handed Rosie her drink. One grabbed an elbow on my way back to Jesús. He was about as stoned as a man could be and remain upright. 'Hey, friend. That your midget?'

'She's a dwarf.' 'She your dwarf?' 'She belongs to Disneyworld.' 'No shit?' 'No shit. Escaped a couple of months ago. Lost her leg to a gator crossing the swamp at night.' 'That's some radical shit, friend. Radical shit.' I leaned between fronds of hair which hung like curtains over a weather worn face. 'Keep it to yourself, my friend. Can't have word get out.' 'I hear you, friend. I hear you.'

Jesús was waiting for me at the counter. 'Hey, Maria. *Mi cabrón*, Three-Piece. *Chido. Él es Irlandés.'* The bartender eyed me as she sparked up a blunt. *'Mi Abuelito estaba Irlandés.* 'No shit! Hear that, Three-Piece. Maria's granddaddy was Irish.' Jesús was so pumped one might have thought Irishmen abroad were a scarce commodity. Maria erupted into rapid Spanish. Turned out Maria's grandaddy's granddaddy was a national hero, an Irish immigrant who had fought for Mexico against America in the 1840s. Second in command to John Riley from Galway. *'Mundo pequeño.'* I said and smiled at Maria. Fatigue was kicking in. I needed a bump. I looked towards the booths and caught a death stare from the rugged bald man. His face looked like it had been hewn from teak with a blunt stone. 'Jesús. The dude over there. What's his story?' Jesús looked at the man and waved. 'That's The Chief', bro. My soul brother, a real live hero right there.' 'Yeah?' 'Hell, yeah! Purple hearts, medals, that hombre did four tours in Vietnam, bro. *Mucho peligroso.* We sit with him, yes?'

I followed Jesús across to the booth. As we sat, The Chief leaned forward and punched Jesús bang on the chin. Jesús crumpled onto the floor, unconscious. I leaned down and put him into recovery position before sitting again. 'I take it that was your gun he took.' 'That's one dumb son of a bitch. He do any damage?' 'I talked him out of it.' 'Sounds like I owe you. Where's the piece?' 'Must be out in the truck.' He slid from the booth, took the keys from Jesús's pocket and strode to the back door. I snuck a bump and watched Rosie reel in the Banditos. Looking for a crate, a short cue, the usual routine to sucker men into throwing dollar bills on the table. The Chief arrived back with two beers, placed one in front of me, and sat down with back to wall. 'I'm Three-Piece.' 'Uku' he said and shook my hand. A deep bullet scar ran the length of a Popeye forearm. He looked to the bikers, gathered laughing around Rosie. One emerged from behind the bar, dropped to one knee and presented her with a beer crate. 'The dwarf. She on the hustle?' 'Yeah.' 'You on a cut?' 'She does her own thing. Think I lose more to her than anybody.'

We watch Rosie's performance. The dragging of the crate, the vault, the seemingly clumsy shot, the lucky pot, the dollar bills landing on the table as all bet against her luck holding out. Uku looks over at me. 'How'd you end up with a name like Three-Piece?' 'Long story.' 'We in a hurry or something?' 'You know what holy communion is?' 'My mother was Catholic, Irish/Mexican.' 'I grew up in an institution.' What kind of institution?' 'An orphanage. When I was eight, I was farmed out to a foster family, the Muldoons, just in time for my first holy communion. Mrs Muldoon decided to dress me up in a three-piece suit for my big day. All the boys were dressed up. Shirt, tie, jacket or whatever. But I was the only one with a waistcoat. I've been known as Three-Piece ever since.' Uku laughed long and hard, body convulsing as he struggled for breath. 'Man, that's some crazy shit. You mean to tell me you've been called Three-Piece since you were eight years old cause you wore a waistcoat?' 'Ireland's like that. Once you get a nickname, it sticks.' 'That must be thirty years?' 'Twenty-nine. Could be worse. She could have dressed me in a frilly blouse.' 'That's a pretty inauspicious start to family life.' 'Didn't end too well either. They signed me into another institution when I was fifteen.'

Jesús stirred on the floor, slowly climbed to his feet, took a few moments to focus on the two of us. 'Hey, Uku. Think I blacked out.' 'It's been a long night, *migo*. Maybe you should lie up for a while.' 'Yeah. Think I might do that.' Jesús stumbles into the next booth and flops down onto the seat. 'You hit him pretty hard.' 'Not really. The candy he was smoking last night wore off, that's all.' 'How'd you end up with a name like The Chief? 'That's my name. Uku is Cherokee for chief. My daddy's side of the family. He had high hopes for me.' 'An Irish/Mexican mother and Cherokee father. Good fighting pedigree.' 'All I've ever been good at.' He took a moment to size me up. 'What are you good at?' 'Surviving.' 'I buy that. Not every man could survive Jesús on a candy rampage.' 'He wanted a way out. I gave it to him. He said you served in Nam.' 'Spent a little time there.' 'That why you can't sleep?' 'Who says I can't sleep?' 'It's past five a.m. and you're drinking alone in the last chance saloon.' 'I can't sleep when my piece is in the hands of a loco Mexican. Had to wait until that motherfucker showed up.' Uku went quiet, scanned the room, watched the Banditos cheer on Rosie as she shaped to pot the black. I waved to Maria and she placed two beers on the counter. I grabbed them and returned to the table, quickly checking on Jesús before sitting down.

'I don't sleep either.' 'You're high on meth, *migo*.' 'That obvious?' 'Might want to wipe the powder ring from your nostril.' I whip a paper napkin from the table dispenser and wipe my nose. 'I mean in general.' 'I know what you mean.' Uku reached into an inside pocket and took out a short pipe and a baggie of weed. He loaded the bowl, sparked a brass Zippo and took a hit. He pushed the makings across the table to me, watched as I repeated the process. 'What has you in Orlando?' 'Took a wrong turn in New York.' 'Took it pretty fast, I reckon. How long you been high?' 'This is day five, I think. Or maybe six. What day is today?' 'Sunday. You might want to sober up if you're going to church.' 'This is church enough for me right now.' 'I hear you, *migo*. The sacred herb will redeem us.' Uku loaded his pipe and took another hit. The bag lady from two booths up appeared, an apparition through his exhaled smoke, clutching her plastic fork like it was the Olympic torch. She looked about eighty, scrawny with a hooked nose and stooped posture. 'Hey Uku. You got any pot to spare?' Uku extracted a couple of buds from his baggie, wrapped them in a paper napkin and handed it to her. 'God bless you, Uku. Happy New Year.' Uku slid across the seat and took the woman in his arms. 'Happy New Year, Gert.' He released her and slid back. Gert pointed her plastic fork at him. '1999 is going to be our year, Uku. I can feel it in my bones.' She turned and hobbled back to her booth. 'What's her story?' 'She took a wrong turn.' He waved at Maria. We sat in silence until she brought our beers to the table and returned to the bar. 'The thing about wrong turns is that you don't know they're wrong when you take those motherfuckers.' 'Amen to that,' I said. We clinked bottles. 'Fucking amen to that.'

Time curled in on itself as we kicked back into the haze to a soundtrack of classic rock and unruly Banditos. We were shaken from our stupor when Rosie hopped over for a bump. I introduced her to Uku. 'You look like one mean Muthafucka. No offence.' 'None taken.' 'Don't worry, honey. I'd still fuck you.' 'That's a weight off my mind, lil lady.' Rosie snorted her bump, shouted 'Muthafucka' and shook her shoulders. 'You want to go back to the motel, soon?' 'Fuck no. I ain't going nowhere. I'm fifteen hundred up and it's not even sunrise.' She bounced back to the Banditos. 'C'mon, you hairy ass pieces of shit. Someone has to give me a game.' Uku chuckled. I snuck a bump, offered him the baggie. He shook his head. 'Done my time with that shit in Nam.' 'How long?' 'Three tours between sixty-seven and seventy-one.' 'Shit deal.' 'That ain't maybe.' 'Different place now.' 'You travelled the region?' 'Yeah. I'm over a couple of times a year. Vietnam, Cambodia, Thailand.' Uku smiles. 'What are you exporting?' 'At the moment, Viagra.' 'You're shitting me?' 'It's twenty-five a pop in Ireland. I can buy it in Phnom Penh for a dollar a pop.' 'The same pills?' 'Indian knock offs but the same drug. No patent laws in India.' 'Why don't you buy them in India?' 'You ever been to India?' 'Can't say that I have.' 'Southeast Asia is a more enjoyable place to do business.' 'How much you sell the pills for?' 'I sell them for between twenty and twenty-five.' 'You're shitting me.' 'Seriously. Availability isn't the issue. Anyone can get them, but nobody wants to go to the doctor and say they can't get it up.' 'What about distribution?' 'My mate's a dealer. He offers them with his other produce, takes five per pill. On average, I clear thirteen to fifteen per tablet after expenses.' 'Man. That's sweet.' 'It won't last forever. Eventually you'll be able to buy that shit over the counter. Keeps me in funds for now, though.' 'What kind of bulk?' 'Took five thousand home last trip. Takes a while to shift, between sixty and eighty per week at the moment, but building all the time.' Uku's brow wrinkled as he did the arithmetic in his head. 'There's a lot of women in Galway who owe me a debt of gratitude. I'll give you my contact if you want.' 'Yeah?' 'Yeah. Not like I'll be bringing the love to Florida. You got a pen?' Uku rummages in a pocket and presents me with an ornate hand-crafted fountain pen. I twirl it in my fingers. 'Nice pen.' 'I like to write.' I tear a napkin from the dispenser and scribble down the details. 'My man's name is Makara. Tell him you're a friend of Three-Piece. I've included my number. If there's any problem, get in contact and I'll vouch for you.' I hand Uku the napkin. He folds it, places it in his breast pocket. 'I sure appreciate that. Could do with a vacation.' 'You shifting weed?' 'A little.' 'Mexico?' 'Mostly my own. I've got me a patch out in the swamp. Getting wild down south. Motherfuckers gone gun crazy. Bringing down all kinds of heat.'

We took another hit and settled into an easy silence. The intro to 'Shine On You Crazy Diamond' was licking the frayed edges of my consciousness when Uku leaned into me. 'When were you diagnosed, *migo*?' 'Four years back. They were treating me for sleep apnoea, 'cause I was waking up choking, you know, not able to breathe.' 'I hear you, *migo*.' 'Nothing did any good, must have been years without a night's sleep.' 'How'd you get diagnosed?' 'Regressive hypnotherapy.' 'You're shitting me?' 'Turned out I was reliving a repressed memory.' 'Yeah? From when?' 'From when I was institutionalised.' 'I take it, it wasn't napalm you were choking on?' 'No. It wasn't napalm.' Rosie vaulted onto the seat. 'Bump me, Muthafucka.' We both snorted a bump. 'I need to crash, Rosie.' 'I ain't goin' nowhere. This place is one sweet deal.' 'You're going to stay in Orlando?' 'Maybe I will. Who the fuck knows? You hit the highway, Three-Piece. I'll catch you up down the road a ways.' Rosie kissed me on the cheek, patted my crotch and swung down off the seat. I watched her hop back to the Banditos, the clack of her shillelagh on the tiled floor contributing off tempo beats to the music. Uku placed his pipe in a jacket pocket and stood. 'You want a ride back to your motel?'

Hatchet and Olivia were sat outside amongst a bunch of pasty tourists when we roared into the motel lot on a 1300cc Fat Boy. I hopped off the pillion seat and fist bumped Uku.

'Later, *migo*,' he said and took off, exhaust cracking like a Gatling gun as he pulled out onto International Drive and sped back towards town. I assumed a nonchalant air and turned to Hatchet and an open-mouthed Olivia. 'Howye.' 'Where were you?' asked Hatchet, looking around at the gathered hicks, self-conscious of what he must look like among the tourists. 'Went for a beer.' 'Yeah? Where?' 'Downtown.' Olivia punches me in the arm. 'We thought you'd crashed, man. Couldn't get no answer when we knocked on the door.' She was saucer-eyed, squawking at me. 'Who's the lad on the bike? Looks like fucking Mike Tyson, man.' 'Uku. He's a mate of mine.' Hatchet wasn't having any of it, knew he'd missed out on an adventure. As he shaped to interrogate me, a Disney shuttle bus pulled up and Olivia dragged him onto it. 'C'mon, man. We'll catch him later, like.' I walked to the room, flopped onto the bed, smiled at the thought of Hatchet spending his entire day at Disney obsessing about what he might have missed. 'It's the simple pleasures,' I mumbled as sleep washed over me. 'It's the simple pleasures.'

Galway. Sprawled stoned across my couch. Watching replays of the twin towers come down. Urgent knocking at the front door. Olivia. Obviously traumatised by events in New York. 'Three-Piece. Have you heard?' 'I'm watching it on TV. Come in.' She followed me into the room as they reran footage of the second plane striking the south tower. It's a long shot this time. We stood silent before the screen for a moment. 'Not this. Hatchet.' 'What about him?' 'He's banged up in *Surat Thani*.' 'Fuck off.' 'Seriously, one of the Thais ratted him out. Shades raided when they were packing the weed.' 'Fuck's sake. Were you talking to him?' 'Last night. He has a deal done with the shades. Twenty in sterling and he cuts them in on the scam. I have it here.' Olivia opened her handbag and bundled £20,000 in English notes onto the coffee table. She placed a smaller wad to one side, along with a white envelope. 'Two grand for expenses, and a one-way ticket to Bangkok. You'll have to book the return for both of you that side. Might look suspicious if you're only staying a few days.' 'Jesus, Olivia. I can't go to Bangkok. I'm up to my eyes.' 'You have to. Hatchet said it had to be you.' I opened the envelope and checked the ticket. 'Tomorrow morning? I need more time than that.' 'There is no time. It has to be sorted in the next three days. He's done a deal with the two that arrested him. Once the regional commander gets back, all bets are off. Hatchet will be sent to the Bangkok Hilton. He'll get twenty years, Three-Piece.' 'The flights are probably grounded.' 'The flight to Bangkok is still going. I checked.' 'Security will be a nightmare. They'll be searching everyone.' Olivia slumped onto the couch and burst into tears.

The following night I was mooching through the humid cacophonic chaos of Khao San Road with a small rucksack over my shoulder and £20,000 strapped to my midriff, paranoid as a one-eyed meerkat in heavy mist, suspicious of every smile from every bargirl, every street vendor. I knew Hatchet hadn't slipped my name, aside from saying Three-Piece on the call to Olivia, but his new business partners could monitor Irish passengers arriving to Bangkok, watch buses and trains to Surat Thani. They could pull me in, take the money, throw both of us into the Bangkok Hilton. Why would they bother? They knew I'd be walking into that police station with the cash. What if one double-crossed the others? Planned to take all of the money for himself?

I spotted Lucky Beer ahead on the right, decided to grab a drink, calm my nerves before heading for the South Terminal to catch the night bus. I ducked through clothing stalls, skirted by an old-timer stir-frying grasshoppers, caught the waspish fumes of garlic and chilli in soy. A hand touched the wad strapped around my waist. I swung my arm back, turned to see a Thai girl tumble into a rack of tie dye sarongs. 'Shit. *Pom Khor Thod.*' I pulled her from her colourful nest, lifted the knocked clothes rail and attempted to rearrange the sarongs. The stall owner, an ancient toothless woman wearing an Iron Maiden T-shirt, ushered me away. I'd caused enough damage. The girl brushed herself down, took my hand and smiled. '*Sawadee Ka.* We go for drink, yes?' '*Mai. Khop khun khap.* I must meet my friend.' Her smile inverted to a cartoon frown. 'Maybe later?' she says. '*Chai.* Later.' I break free of her grip, catch her glance at my midriff as I turn away.

Lucky Beer hadn't changed. Same DJ banging out tunes, sweaty *farangs* throwing back cocktails, locals distributing food and drink. The room was building a head of steam. In another hour, all would spill dancing onto the street. I planned to be gone by then. I climbed the steps to the upper level in search of a seat and spotted the bald dome of Uku in a darkened corner. He tipped his bottle of *Chang* in my direction, as if expecting me. I sat beside him, facing the room. '*Sawadee Kap, migo.*' 'Hey, Uku.' I asked a passing waiter for two Chang, looked up to the TV screen facing our corner. The twin towers were still collapsing. 'Sorry bout the shite in New York.' 'We had it coming, *migo*, we had it coming this long while.' The waiter placed two beers on paper napkins, along with a small bowl of nuts. 'Rosie's dead.' 'No way.' ''Fraid so, *migo*. Freak accident.' 'Hit her head doing backflips?' 'How the fuck do you know that?' 'An accident waiting to happen. When did she...'

'Bout eighteen months ago. She'd been living with me, rented my spare room since that morning in The Pit. Quite the character.' 'She was that.' 'Sorry, *migo*. Should have let you know.' 'Makes no odds. Not like I could have come over for the funeral or anything.' 'She loved you, *migo*. Three-Piece is kind, she used to say. Three-Piece is one kind Muthafucka. He just won't admit it. Reckon she expected you to walk into The Pit some morning and offer her a lift back to New York.' 'Would she have gone back?' 'No. She just wanted to tell you to go fuck yourself.' We laughed, clinked our bottles. 'To Rosie.'

We observed the room for a few moments, the carefree vibe of the tourists in stark contrast to the twin towers collapsing again and again on multiple screens. 'We gave her quite the farewell.' 'Yeah?' 'Yeah. She was right popular downtown, despite being contrary as a gator with toothache. Found close to fifteen thousand dollars in her room. Weren't nobody to send it to. She never spoke of family, never received no post. Hell. I didn't even know her last name.' 'It was a Polish name,' I said. 'Kowalski or something... What'd you do with the cash?' 'Threw a three-day party at The Pit, with Rosie's casket on a pool table, then buried her in Greenwood Cemetery.' 'Greenwood?' 'The most upmarket cemetery in Florida. Tree-lined avenues, landscaped gardens, where all the rich folk bury their kin. You'd wanna see the looks on their faces when two-hundred Banditos thundered through the manicured grounds towing Rosie's casket. Them folks didn't know what the fuck was going on.' I laughed at the vision of Rosie's final journey, creating one last crazy scene on her way out. 'I had her headstone erected a couple of months back.' 'Yeah? What's the inscription?' 'Here lies Rosie. Super Sharp Shooter.' 'She'd love that.' 'I reckon so, *migo*. I reckon so.' Uku slapped my shoulder and walked towards the toilets. I ordered another couple of beers, watched the room slide towards debauchery. A pang of loneliness shot through me. I may have never seen Rosie again, but it was comforting to know she was out in the world somewhere, shooting pool in a sleazy bar, cracking skulls with her shillelagh, willing to go wherever the night might lead.

Uku returned as the waiter placed our beers on the table. 'Makara said you'd been in touch.' 'Makara's one straight up *hombre.*' 'He's a sound head, alright. You loaded up?' 'Loaded up with nowhere to go.' He points his bottle at the TV screen. 'I switched to the gel. Cheaper, easier to transport. Then this shit goes down.' He takes a swig, laughs. 'Is what it is, *migo.* I'll treat it as an opportunity for an extended vacation. Your snow-white complexion tells me you're just off the plane.' 'Arrived a few hours ago. Mate's banged up in *Surat Thani.*' 'You here to pay off the cops?' 'Yeah. Twenty grand and he cuts them in on the deal.' 'They know you're here?' 'Don't think so. Three-Piece ain't the name on my passport.' 'Anybody else know?' 'A girl outside. Patted me down from behind.' 'That's a potential complication, *migo.* You travelling tonight?' 'Going to grab the night bus.' 'You're going to walk into crooked cops carrying twenty grand?' 'Don't have much choice.' 'Sounds like you're in need of a wing man.' 'Since you're not busy...' 'You got it, *migo.* I'm in the mood for a moonlit drive.' 'Hope you're not getting any romantic notions.' 'Maybe I am, *migo.* The tropics do strange things to a man.' 'I'll take my chances.'

We throw back our beers, chase them with a couple of Red Bulls and leave through the back door. Uku leads the way through a succession of narrow streets, passing the street food market before hanging a left onto *Soi Kraisi.* A couple of hundred metres up the street, a teenage Thai boy sits on a chopped Harley loaded with large pannier bags and a bedroll.

Uku high fives the boy, hands him fifty baht, takes a key from his pocket and starts up the bike. Its feral roar draws all attention to us. Groups of youngsters point and gather round. Uku looks to me. 'Mount up, *migo*.' I climb onto the pillion seat and we take off, thundering through side streets, weaving through tuk tuks, cars, bicycles, trucks, pedestrians and scooters. Carcinogenic humidity gave way to a fragrant breeze as we left the chaos of Bangkok behind and headed south on the highway.

We drove through the night, the low guttural growl of the chopper our soundtrack, stopping to refuel, knock back Red Bull and share spliffs 'to take the edge off'. As we approached Surat Thani, flamingo-pink bands spread across the sky by the rising sun distracted from my sore backside. Macaques watched us pass from undergrowth at the edge of the treeline. The resigned expression on their wizened faces seemed ominous. I inhaled deep of the salt air, watched a fish eagle thread thermals overhead, fingered the cash strapped to my waist. The police station was on Namueang Road, near the harbour, a white rectangular two-story with a line of fluttering flags and a large forecourt. We drove by, pulled over by the river a couple of streets away, spent twenty minutes or so stretching by a bench. None of the passers-by paid us any mind. Just another couple of *farangs* in town to catch a ferry to Samui. I sat on the bench, ripped the wads from my waistband and placed them in a khaki knapsack Uku threw at my feet. I left my small rucksack beside it. 'I'll text once I know it's safe.' 'I'll be here, *migo*.'

The police station stank of carbolic acid. I pulled the slip of paper which Olivia had given me from my wallet and approached a battle-scarred bamboo counter, behind which sat an equally battle-scarred officer. He watched me approach, expressionless, oblivious to the choking fumes. 'I'm looking for Sergeant Huang.' He stared. My eyes strayed to the stripes on the short sleeves of his pressed shirt. I yanked my T-shirt up over my nose for fear of passing out. 'Snakes,' he said, and leaned back in his chair, as if that solitary noun explained everything. 'Sergeant Huang?' 'You Ireland man?' 'Irish. Yes. I'm here to see my friend.' A tailless gecko dropped from the ceiling, landed on the counter, scurried off, flopped onto the floor, froze. I watched its skin turn the off-white hue of the tiles. 'You Ireland?' 'Yes.' He turned his head and barked an instruction in Thai. Another officer emerged from a door to the rear of the room. The sergeant stood, grabbed a wooden truncheon. His colleague replaced him at the counter. 'Come with me.'

I followed the sergeant into a tiny room to one side of the reception area, bare aside from three rickety chairs and a Formica-topped desk. He closed the door, clunked his truncheon onto the desk, and turned to face me. The stench was worse in the tiny space. He watched me pull my tee-shirt higher over my nose. 'Snakes' he said. 'You have money?' 'Yes.' He looked me up and down, obviously expecting me to present him with the money. 'I have the money.' I placed my phone and wallet on the desk by the truncheon, pulled out my pockets. 'But not here. I bring when I see my friend.' He took a few seconds to register what I'd said, walked behind me and patted me down, stood back and glared. A long silence was punctuated by a disjointed rhythm of horns blaring from the street, the chatter of parakeets from outside the barred window. 'Your friend. Snake man.' He seemed to be expecting a response. 'My friend?' 'Yes. Your friend. Snake man.'

I was sleep deprived, had glugged Red Bull and smoked Thai weed for the past ten hours. Was it possible a Surat Thani police sergeant was telling me Hatchet had morphed into a reptilian superhero? Seemingly losing patience with my flawed comprehension, the sergeant marched from the room. He returned half a minute later clutching a dead king cobra. He flung it onto the floor at my feet. It was a prize specimen, about six foot in length with a thick muscular body. 'Your friend.' He bent down, gripped the cobra's tail, swung it around and whacked its head off the wall. 'Your friend. Snake man.' He laughed, which heightened my fear that not only had I no idea of what was going on, there was little chance of me leaving this stinking cess pit alive. The carbolic acid was obviously to dispose of bodies, the cobra a symbol of what had been done to Hatchet. They had killed a serpent. They were about to kill me.

I smiled, bowed slightly, so the sergeant would relax. I was a second away from throwing a straight right to his chin and making a grab for the truncheon when Hatchet's flatulent cackle pulsed from reception. He sauntered into the room, accompanied by a giggling officer. The sergeant poked my ribs. 'Your friend. Snake man.' Hatchet fist bumped me as if we'd just met on a Galway side street. 'Three-Piece. You took your time. He consulted his bare wrist. You travel by boat or what?' The two police officers cracked up. Hatchet had obviously become Mr Popular. He placed a hand on my shoulder. *'Ar thug tú an spondoolies?' 'Sea. Suas an bóthar.'* Hatchet looked at the sergeant. 'My friend. He has the money. He gets, yes?' The sergeant nodded. Hatchet pointed at the door. 'Go get the dosh. It's cool.'

I left the station and walked to where Uku lay stretched upon the bench, khaki knapsack beneath his bald head. 'You cool, *migo*?' 'Think so. Weird as fuck in there.' 'Suppose you'll be wanting my pillow.' 'I'll be back with it shortly. I hope.'

'Yeah, well I know where to find you if you ain't.' I returned to the station. The officer at the counter didn't even look up, so I crossed reception and entered the small room. Hatchet and the two officers were sat around the desk shooting the breeze. Hatchet rose from his seat as I entered and took the knapsack from my hand. He unzipped it, peered inside, placed the wads on the desk. 'Now if you gentlemen would be kind enough to give me a receipt, I'll be on my way.' A moment of silence before the three exploded into laughter. The sergeant caught my eye, pointed at Hatchet. 'Your friend. Snake man.' I laughed, anxious to maintain the positive vibe in the room. Hatchet shook hands with the officers. 'C'mon,' he said, and threw the knapsack to me. The sergeant stood. 'Wait.' He picked up the cobra and handed it to Hatchet. 'For you, yes.' *'Kap Khun Kap.'* said Hatchet and accepted the gift.

We walked towards the river, me with the knapsack over my shoulder, Hatchet with the dead king cobra slung around his neck. 'What's with the "snake man" shite?' 'I killed the cobra. Came into my cell night before last.' 'How'd you kill it?' 'Charmed it.' 'Charmed it?' 'Yep. Got it nice and relaxed, like, then grabbed it by the throat and smashed its head off the wall. The Thais are scared shitless of cobras. The sergeant arrived in with breakfast yesterday, I had the cobra draped over the bars. Thought I was a mighty man altogether. Sorry I didn't hide the fucking thing; they dosed the whole place with carbolic acid, nearly suffocated me with the fumes.' 'When did you add snake charmer to your CV?' 'I've had to charm a lot of snakes this past week. The cobra was the easiest of them.'

We heard the throb of Uku's chopper before we reached the river. He had a local boy sitting on the seat, twisting the throttle. The boy looked about eight, obviously buzzed by the experience of revving a Harley. He was even more excited to see the king cobra around Hatchet's neck. He pointed, leapt off the bike. '*Naja. Naja.*' 'Hatchet, Uku.' 'Hey, Uku.' 'Pleased to make your acquaintance, *migo*. That's quite the necklace.' Hatchet gripped Uku's outstretched hand; adopted a Thai accent. 'They're doing "very special price" down at the station.' Hatchet squinted at Uku. 'I've seen you before.' 'Not in your dreams, I hope.' 'Orlando,' I said. 'Uku dropped me back to the motel. On the Harley.' 'I have you now. How's Rosie?' 'Rosie's dead, *migo*.' 'Sorry to hear that. Back-flips?' Uku looked at me. 'You guys never think to advise Rosie against that particular endeavour?' 'Rosie wasn't one for heeding advice.' I said. '*Naja. Naja.*' Hatchet took the snake from around his neck and held it out to the boy. 'You want?' The boy looked at Hatchet, down at the snake, back up at Hatchet. The morning had shaped to be the most eventful of his life thus far. He eased his two hands forward. Hatchet draped the cobra over skinny trembling arms, wound the tail around his wrists. The boy smiled, then ran across the narrow road and ducked down a side street. Hatchet laughed at the sight of him straining under the weight of the snake. 'Off to tell his mates he killed a cobra. He'll be known as Snake Boy.' I wanted to call after the boy, advise him to stop, warn him how difficult it is to lose a nickname once it sticks.

Uku scanned the street before turning to Hatchet. 'You clear, *migo*?' 'I'm clear. Better off than before. They'll handle the shipping from here on. Well worth cutting them in.' 'Sweet deal.' 'They'll fuck me eventually, but it'll do for now.' Hatchet grabbed me in a head lock. 'Thanks for coming down, you fucker.' He released me and punched me in the ribs, his favoured expression of gratitude. 'What now?' I asked. 'My gear's over in Hat Salat. May as well head there and chill for a few days before heading back. We can book a flight from

Samui.' 'What about you, Uku? There's a hammock on Koh Phangan with your name on it.' 'That sounds mighty tempting, *migos*, but I was heading north when Three-Piece showed up in need of a travelling companion. Think I might get myself back in that direction.' 'Here.' Hatchet roots around in the pockets of his sleeveless jacket and pulls out a business card. This is the best hostel in Chang Rai. Ask for Ah Nong, tell her you're a mate of Hatchet. She'll look after you. Has a great suss on the Lahu tribe if you fancy heading into the hills for an opium dream. They'll lock up the bike while you're gone.' 'That sounds mighty fine. I'll check it out.' Uku pockets the card, goes to shake my hand. 'A pleasure crossing paths again, Three-Piece.' I pulled him into a hug. 'You should come to Galway for a visit. We'll show you a good time.' He broke the embrace, mounted the chopper, started up. 'That's what I'm afraid of.' He clunked into first. 'Catch you down the road, *migos*.' We watched Uku speed off towards the highway. 'Where'd you bump into him?' 'Lucky Beer.' 'He's the real deal, that lad.' Hatchet poked me. 'Give me your phone. Better ring Livi and tell her we'll be home in a few days.

. . .

Hatchet conked in the passenger seat within fifteen minutes of leaving Dublin airport. The peace was a soothing balm. The mad bastard hadn't shut up since we left Samui. He'd scored yaba in Hat Rin just before we caught the ferry and couldn't resist dropping '...so we can have a good chat on the way home, like.' When we transferred in Bangkok, I gave in and dropped myself, if only to keep my ears up to speed. I was on the verge of jitters when we landed, so augmented my dose to get me through the drive to Galway. The radio spouted nothing but post 9/11 tripe. I knocked it off and drove in silence, the ghosts of road trips past intruding on my mangled thoughts. We'd just passed Athlone when I saw Rosie backflipping down the dual carriageway ahead of the car, shillelagh tucked tight beneath her right arm. I followed her onto the exit for Ballinasloe, through three roundabouts, took a left, a right, pulled up in front of white wrought iron gates set into a limestone arch. Through the gates, Rosie backflipped around a familiar courtyard, into the panoptic arms of the sprawling limestone building, its white front door stark beneath an imposing clock tower. I watched her swing her shillelagh as she backflipped along the front facade, smashing small square panes set in large Georgian windows, back and forth, back and forth, until all the panes were broken. She stopped at the front door, raised her shillelagh, turned towards me, and smiled.

'Three-Piece! Three-Piece!' Hatchet shouting beside me. 'What?' 'You're asleep, you fucker.' 'No, I'm not.' 'You were snoring, for fuck's sake. What are we doing here? They built the bypass for good reason, you know.' I read the plaque set into the left pillar.

BORD SLÁINTE AN IARTHAIR – OSPIDÉAL NAOMH BRID.

WESTERN HEALTH BOARD – ST BRIGID'S HOSPITAL.

'Three-Piece! You alright?' 'They took psychiatric out of the name.' 'It was never in the name, not in our time.' 'You sure?' 'It's been St Brigid's Hospital since the fifties. Fuck this shithole. It's in the past.' The two of us sat in silence, looking through the gates at the abandoned building, its windows intact, its clocktower silhouetted against a shepherd's sky the hue of a fresh scab. Hatchet touched my elbow. 'We've come a long way.' 'We're four feet from the front gate.' I reversed onto the road, drove through the roundabouts, back onto the bypass. Hatchet glanced sideways at me as I shifted through the gears and got up to speed. 'You know what I mean,' he said. 'Yeah. I know what you mean.'

ACKNOWLEDGEMENTS

To all the rogues, chancers, misfits and crazy diamonds for their splendid company on the wild trips.

To the Gannon family, for placing a shovel in my hand any time I got notions.

I owe a debt of gratitude to Adrian Frazier and John Kenny for taking the time to shine coal. To the storytellers of Galway, far too many to name, for setting a high bar in those low places we like to frequent. My co-vagabond, John O'Dowd, with whom I sit back and watch the money roll in. My sister, Judith, for keeping the home fire burning. My fellow scribblers in the Atlantis Collective; Aideen Henry, Dara O'Foglu, Trish Holmes, Colm Brady, Alan Caden, Paul McMahon, and Maire Robinson. I'd better thank John Donnellan (JD), as he features in three stories and may sue me. Mick Friel, who features in 'Shadows', and Domo Lally, whose dog gets a mention. Kitty Harris, whose childhood experiences inspired 'Distilling'. The bould Ray Kelly, the raconteur from whom I steal the most. The Commander, for his psychedelic cockroach. Olaf Tyaransen, for his feedback and encouragement; Kevin Healy, who gave me my first laptop 'to write that damn book'. Cian Campbell, who kept me in nixers. The main dealer, Vincenzo Browne. The man who won't take yes for an answer, Seamus

Ruttledge, and the late Mark Kennedy for insisting I 'keep it real, man.' *Grá agus Solas.*

Special mention to those writers who generously took time out from their own work to read this collection prior to publication: Aoibheann McCann, Martina Evans, Mike McCormack, Elaine Feeney, Órfhlaith Foyle, Emer Martin, Alan McMonagle and Jess Kidd. It's my round for the foreseeable future.

To David Borrowdale at Reflex Press, for his encouragement at the early stages of this endeavour, and his remarkable patience throughout the process. It requires a special brand of cool to survive the transition from GMT to 'Galway time'. Respect.

To all with London Writers' Eclective for their support and inspiration. My co-director and collaborator, Lindsey Booth; Sue Olney, Rose Van Orden, Jonny Anderson, Radmila Sarac, Lindsay Taylor, Veronica Robinson, Vince Love, Rachel Moorhead, Mick Durham, Liam Nwanze, Geeta Sanker, Melanie Johnson, Aileen O'Farrell, Jenn Murray, Kieran Kelliher, Veronica Flanagan, Wendy Fisher, Carolyn Gaunt, Ian Pollock, Francis O'Flynn, Margaret Rochford, Simon Roberts, Ginny Griffin Monk, Helen Cylwik, Gail Golding, Judi Bevan, Louise Kosinska, Kevin Stewart, Carl Brady, Luke Aldridge, Polly Taylor, Neil Roberts, Margaret Mentzer, Mark Dwyer, Maeve Curry, Patrick Clifton.

To the London posse for their support; Mark Isherwood, Linda Quinn, William Foote, Gavin Clarke, Ros Scanlan, Dorothy Allen, Peter Power-Hynes, the late David O'Keeffe and Carina Monckton.

Last but by no means least, the late Mary Montague, who kept me fed, watered and inspired while I was digging for gold.

. . .

The author and publisher wish to thank the editors of the publications in which the following stories first appeared, online or in print:

'Kindle' first appeared in *The Real Jazz Baby – Reflex Fiction Volume Two*, July 2019; 'The Bat Man of Hat Salat' – *Survival: Award Winning Short Stories*, September 2021; 'The Integrity of Cockroaches' – *Shooter Literary Magazine*, January 2017; 'Star Cross'd' – *Beguiled by a Wild Thing – Reflex Fiction Volume Four*, June 2021; 'Sacred Streams of Balaji Dham' – *Flash Fiction Magazine*, October 2019; 'Nothing to Be Done' – *The Writers' Bureau*, May 2019; 'Capital Vices' – *The Lonely Crowd*, September 2023; 'Shadows' – *Noir by Noir West: Dark Fiction from the West of Ireland*, May 2014; 'Flashes' – *Sticks and Stones: An Oxford Flash Fiction Anthology*, April 2022; 'Gravediggers' – *Snow Crow – Bath Flash Fiction Volume Six*, December 2021; 'Galway City: Christmas Eve 1974' – *Reflex Fiction*, November 2018; 'Eating Swans' – *Galway Stories*, April 2013; 'Uffizi' – *The Real Jazz Baby – Reflex Fiction Volume Two*, July 2019; 'Kind of Blue' – *A Girl's Guide to Fly Fishing – Reflex Fiction Volume Three*, July 2020; 'All Roads Lead to Ballinasloe' – *HOWL: New Irish Writing*, October 2023.

REFLEX PRESS

Reflex Press is an independent publisher based in Abingdon, Oxfordshire, committed to publishing bold and innovative books by emerging authors from across the UK and beyond.

Since our inception in 2018, we have published award-winning short story collections, flash fiction anthologies, and novella-length fiction.

www.reflex.press
@reflexfiction